Old World Pharmaceuticals

BRIAN MYRICK

DEDICATION

This book is dedicated to the three woman that mean the world to me.

Vivian Philips

Samantha Myrick-Reynolds

Tamsen Bridges-Myrick

TABLE OF CONTENTS

CHAPTER ONE

The Year Is 1985

The full moon rises into the night sky and the world is quiet. It's late into the night and there is a cool breeze blowing now that its late fall. Three men dressed in nice suits and two women in business suits stand in an empty and desolate parking lot in front of a large building that houses a dairy farm office. The sign on the door to the building reads Old World Dairy Farm. The building is located a good way outside of Houston, Texas, but this late at night the tiny lights of the city can still be seen far off in the distance. Blinking and flickering as the city moves through the night. Under a dim parking lot lamppost, all five can be seen holding champagne glasses preparing to toast them.

Azreal, a stern looking and powerfully built man in his early thirties, with sharp eyes, and a worldly presents about him says. "We have all been in this world for a long, long time with nothing to offer it; all we have done is take from it, some of us more than others, but it is time we started giving back to this world."

Samuel, in his mid-thirties a tall slender man, with a pale and defined face and sharp jawlines to match his nose. His strong large hands wrapped around his glass while he takes a sip from it then says, "Now that we have learned what we are actually capable of, there is no need for us to live in the shadows anymore. We can finally coexist with the humans."

The third male, Gabriel, looks to be in his late twenties, small and quick, dark of face, with restless eyes that darting back and forth always looking at what is around him, and a sly smile. He walks away from the others and looks at the building, "Do you really think now is the time for this new beginning, the switch from cattle to pharmaceuticals? Humans won't accept us after they find out how we have lived all these years, even with these new gifts that you want to give them. We have always lived in the shadows, and it has served us well."

Samantha, female, tall with long black hair, in her early twenty's and a body meant for a swimsuit, "There is no chance that humans will forgive me for the crimes I've caused against their race."

"This is a big move, but we have to evolve, or we will die," says Haley, a female, cute with an average build for a woman in her early thirty's, nothing particularly stands out with her, she could easily be walked past in public and never noticed unless you know her, says as she turns toward the other two. "The world has changed around us, and we haven't changed; it's time. To really make this work, it will take a much larger workforce than the cattle dairy and require a lot more trust in our new human friends."

Gabriel turns back towards the group and walks up to Haley, then pats her on the shoulder before taking his spot next to her. She glares at him. Gabriel rolls his eyes and looks at the others.

"Here is a thought, why don't we evolve into the kings and queens of this world?" Gabriel says.

"Enough Gabriel, we have heard and seen this from you for hundreds of years now!" Azreal snaps at him. "We will eventually be caught robbing humans and feeding or killing them. Those days are past us now. We must help each other and change our ways if we want to survive."

With super speed, Azreal moves across the parking lot to stand next to Gabriel and puts a firm hand on his shoulder. Azreal looks deep into Gabriel's eyes. "We have overlooked your indiscretions and frequent rule-breaking for many years now. You have placed all of us in jeopardy many times. You need this new venture and to co-exists with humans most of all, to control the urges I know you struggle with."

Gabriel puts his head down in shame and remorse, then gathers himself and looks back into Azreal's eyes. "I will go along with these new beginnings for the good of the group, but I will never trust humans."

"Then we agree," Samuel says, as he turns to look at Haley, "Start the steps necessary to move forward with us leaving the cattle business. Azreal and I will continue to make new human friends who can help us along the way."

"Even with our new friends, this will still take time to get going," Haley says.

Samantha chuckles and rolls her eyes, then looks over to Gabriel, "All we have is time..."

Azreal with his hand still on Gabriel's shoulder guides him back to the group. All five stand in a semicircular facing each other. With the crickets chirping endlessly in the cool night, and the sound of leaves rustling on the trees as the breeze blows past them.

"Then, let us all toast to this new start," Azreal says as he lifts his glass once more into the air.

"Yes, before our drinks get cold!" Samantha says.

The others raise their glasses up to meet Azreal's toast. Samantha drinks vigorously and some of her glasses contents runs down her chin in a single dark red line of blood. She quickly wipes the drop with her finger, then licks it off the tip of her finger with a smile.

All five of them finish their drinks and begin walking away from the building. At the edge of the parking lot is a large steel dumpster. As they pass by it they throw their glasses into the open dumpster. The glasses, each drained completely, land with a crash as they break on the trash inside. Behind the parking lot is a long pipe fence that holds cattle inside of it. On the other side of the fence, a large strong bull lays on the grass motionless, lifeless, still bleeding out from the gaping wound in his neck. Next to the bull on the soft green grass is an empty champagne glass' box.

* * *

The Year is 2018

On an evening with a sky full of clouds, two black, four-door sedans with federal license plates pull into a parking lot past the dumpster and the long pipe fence that still holds cows inside of it. The doors slam as two occupants leave the vehicles at the same time, Dan

Miller and Frank Garcia. Dan in his mid-40s, stocky and strong but slightly overweight, starting to show the signs of his age with a receding hairline and a weathered face that has seen many summers. Dan walks away from his car first, carrying a thick, brown folder tight to his body. He starts to make his way to the front door of the building. The sign on the front door now reads Old World Pharmaceuticals.

The much younger agent in training, Frank, has a thin and wiry stature, with an eager to impress expression written all over his face as he, follows and hurries to catch up with Dan at the front door of Old World. They both shake off the chill brought in by a gust of wind as the doors to the building slide open for them.

"Wait up Dan, they're not going anywhere," Frank says once he gets behind Dan in the entryway.

"Get a move on Fucking New Guy," Dan says and increases his walking speed to enter the building.

The two of them enter the Old World Pharmaceuticals lobby and look around. At the other end of the lobby is a reception desk, sitting behind the desk is a young woman in her early 20s. She is intently watching the news on a wall-screen TV in the adjacent waiting area. She hardly notices Dan and Frank walk in as they walk up to the receptionist's desk, and Dan sets his folder down with a thud.

“Hello, Ma’am. We have an appointment with your bosses. We’re with the FDA.,” Dan says in a deeper than normal and stern voice.

The receptionist breaks away from the news she is watching on the TV to notice Dan and Frank standing in front of her. Dan flips open his wallet to show her the badge inside of it. Then quickly flips it back shut and slides it back into his pocket.

“Oh, sorry,” the receptionist says, “I was just waiting to see if there are any new leads with that news story.”

Frank leans around Dan to look at the receptionist. He looks at her with curious eyes then gives her a slight smile. She returns it.

“Are you talking about the missing-person story?” Frank asks while he turns to observe the television for a moment.

“It’s the only story on the news now, and it’s not a missing-person case anymore, it’s a missing people case. Have you even been watching it?” The receptionist looks away from Dan and Frank for a moment and out the large, glass window next to her. Off on the horizon, the sun is beginning to set.

The receptionist looks back and down at her scheduling book. There is only one entry in the book that reads Meeting with Food and Drug Administration Agents. Then the receptionist looks back up at

Dan and Frank. "You guys are early," she says and closes the scheduling book. "You can just wait in the waiting area. I'm sure they will see you in a minute."

Dan and Frank walk over and take a seat in the waiting area and start to watch the TV while they wait for the meeting. On the TV screen a silly commercial with a clown and kids playing at a new indoor entertainment center opening in Houston.

The news comes back on with the news anchor saying, "We have a live update on the latest in a series of missing persons reported. Let's go live now, to the Houston PD."

The news program cuts to a briefing area in the Houston Police Department, a public relations officer walks to the podium and sets down some papers, then thumbs through them. His face is concerned and focused. "Good evening, everyone," the officer says after clearing his throat. "I wish I had something better to tell you, but we are still working with the leads we have and there are no new developments in the missing person cases of Vivian Leigh, Liz Reed and Ruby Thomas."

"Can you tell us anything else? Do you think these cases are connected?" a reporter's voice asks loudly over the chatter of the crowd in the briefing room.

“That’s a good question, and we are exploring that possibility also, we are working on every possible lead,” the officer answers, “but what I can tell you is the full resources of our department are being utilized, and we are hopeful that all three of these young women will be found alive and well. I’m sorry, but that is really all I have for you now.” The news cuts back to the regular newsroom and the news anchor.

Back in the lobby of Old World Pharmaceuticals, “Wow, so it’s up to three people now,” Frank exclaims.

Listening to Frank the receptionist shouts over to him “It’s three now but there was, I think, three other girls about a year ago. Yeah, three. I know it’s going to be the same guy.”

“You think so?” Frank shouts back.

“You aren’t here to gossip about the news with the secretary,” Dan says and gives Frank a stern eye.

Frank looks away from the receptionist and back at the TV, the room goes silent, except for the TV playing in the background. The sun is all but gone now; a fading, hazy light on the horizon is all that is left of the day.

The receptionist's phone rings and she answers it. "Yes, Sir. I will show them in." The receptionist hangs up the phone and stands up from her desk. "They're ready for you two, follow me, please."

They walk through a doorway and up a small flight of stairs where the receptionist leads them past a room lined with desks and chairs, all of them empty and old. Some old lab equipment is placed in the corner of the room also.

"This building is pretty big for being out here in the middle of nowhere," Frank says to the receptionist.

"Yes, it is huge," the receptionist says, "but I haven't seen most of it; it's off-limits to the regular employees because that is where they do all the lab work, and I think there is even a basement too. This used to be just a dairy farm a long time ago."

"A dairy farm, like, with cows?" Frank asks.

"That's what would be on a dairy farm," the receptionist says with a smile and a giggle. "Didn't you see some of the cows when you pulled up?"

"Well yes, but I didn't really think about them," Frank replies.

"Come on," Dan says to Frank as Dan picks up his walking pace to get in front of the receptionist.

They continue to walk down long hallways and then come to an elevator at a dead end to the hallway. The elevator doors open, and they step in. The receptionist presses the top button and the elevator rises to the eighth floor.

As the elevator opens, there is a hallway with offices on both sides of it. Beyond that the hallway leads to two large double doors, reinforced with steel, as one might see in an old castle, solid and thick.

"Right through those doors, gentlemen," the receptionist says.

Dan and Frank walk down the hallway and stop at the double doors, "Those are quite the doors," Frank says as he runs his fingers along the intricate iron designs mounted to the heavy wood doors. The doors open from the inside startling Frank and reviling a large room.

Dan and Frank enter the vastness of the conference room. An oval table made of thick solid looking wood occupies the middle of the room all through the table is a detailed and intricate carving with many layers of clear polyurethane on top to protect it. Beyond the table is a patio with a view of the city lights of Houston, far off in the distance. Above the patio windows and door, are steel rolling shutters that can be closed during the day to block the sunlight and for security also. Every wall in the room has large pieces of artwork that looked like it should have been in a museum. Separating the art is dark cherry wood panels and columns that matched the intricate woodworking on the ceiling.

Seated at the back side of the table in oversized, plush red chairs are Gabriel, Haley, and Azreal, who all look the exact same as they did thirty-three years ago in the parking lot of their building. But Samuel, is now noticeably older, he looks to be in his late 60s, and Steven O'Hara, a man in his late 40s, glasses, average build but from his looks, he obviously doesn't own a gym membership, are also seated at the table.

"Good evening, gentleman," Steven says, "please have a seat, and we can get started with this meeting."

Dan and Frank make their way to the table and sit down, in regular cheap office chairs on the other side of the table. Dan opens his brown folder and pulls out several neatly organized stacks of papers, then sets them out in front of him in the precise places he wants them, neat and orderly. Then checks them again so the papers are straight, lined up and spaced equally from each other. Dan looks the papers over while he slowly rolls the fingers of his right hand on the table. Index, middle, ring, pinky finger. Slow gentle thuds on the table. Index, middle, ring, pinky finger. Over and over.

"So, you guys have produced several very impressive drugs, since what, I think 1986?" Dan asks. "That's a long time, I'm sure your shareholders are very happy with your work."

"You know, this is a privately-owned company," Azreal says as he looks up from Dan's compulsiveness of rolling his fingers on the desk. "We took this meeting in hopes of resolving whatever concerns you have and moving forward with our work. I am sure you can see the need for this medication to get to the people that need it quickly."

Dan looks up from his papers at Azreal with a cold, hard stare. Everyone on the other side of the table is watching Dan's every movement as if they were vultures waiting for a meal.

"I know more than anyone else what it means for children to get the medicine they need," Dan says and looks back down at his papers again, continuing to slowly roll his fingers on the table, then, he suddenly looks up at the group again. "You know what? I have a question. It's a question I have had for a long time. Why do you only make limited amounts of these miracle drugs? None of your listed ingredients in any of your drugs is in short supply, so why can't you make more? Why haven't you made more?"

"That is company business," Haley scruffs, "and I don't see any need to discuss that in this setting. We were under the impression your agency had questions about our new drug, XP1, that we would be able to clear up for you."

"You're right," Dan says. "We do have some questions about that, also. So, no answer on why you only make small batches, huh? And why you only let certain doctors administer your drugs? Nah? I didn't think you would have much to say about that, but okay."

The room is quiet while Dan looks from person to person, waiting for an answer. Nothing. They all look at him with blank stares, waiting for him to make the next move.

"Come on, guys this company was on fire," Dan says and raises his eyebrow towards them. "One unexplained, new miracle drug after another for years. Then, nothing for the last 10 years? What happened? Did you just decide you made enough money and quit? Did all of you just go on vacation?" Dan sitting in silence staring at the other side of the table, waiting for some kind of response, any response, but nothing comes. "Nothing again huh? okay."

"This clearly isn't the meeting we were expecting," Haley says then sighs. "I think it's better if we terminate this meeting now, and I refer you to our legal department."

Dan says, "Yeah, I have spoken with them numerous times and they are about as helpful as ya'll are being." The slow rolling of his fingers on the desk are steadily landing with more and more force. Harder and harder each time. Frank slides a stack of the papers in front of Dan over and places them in front of himself and begins to look them over. Dan looks at Frank annoyed.

"So, let's get back to the ingredient list that you submitted to the FDA with your preliminary samples for XP1," Dan says changing the topic. "When examining the compound that you sent, we were able to identify all the ingredients on your list with the exception of what we believe to be one or two extra substances, that are not on your list. Could you possibly have sent us an incomplete list?"

"No, the compound list that was submitted with the samples was complete," Steven O'Hara says. "I'm sure if you test it again, you will find that you have made a mistake."

"Did Director Barker review your finding?" Azreal asks. "I am sure when you retest and submit it to the director, it will contain exactly what we listed."

"It looks like ya'll should have taken a shorter vacation," Dan smirks. "Director Barker was in an auto accident about two years ago and passed away. Our new Director did review our finding, and that is why we are talking to ya'll now."

"What is the new director's name?" Azreal asks.

“It’s her name now. Her name is Angela Thomson,” Frank says.

Frank gets a card out of his wallet and passes it across the table to Azreal. Azreal looks at the card. It reads "Agent in Charge, Angela Thomson." Azreal smiles while looking at the card then looks back at Dan.

“So, Angela Thomson is now the Director?” Azreal asks as his grin grows wider.

Dan glancing through some papers still in front of him stops and looks up at Azreal. Frank can see the hostility growing in Dan’s eyes.

“Do you know her?” Dan asks impatiently.

“Yes, I believe we met some time ago,” Azreal says.

“Really?” Dan asks.

Changing the subject, Azreal asks “Steven, could you please review the list that was sent over to the FDA again to make sure there are no errors.”

“Yes, no problem sir,” Steven says. “I will review what was submitted and look for any possible mistake in the compound list, but I’m sure it was correct.”

"Thanks, but that still doesn't explain why we weren't able to identify what those other compounds are?" Frank says. "Would you mind telling me what they are?"

Frank puts the paper he is holding down and fumbles to take a pen out of his jacket. Then, he looks back at Steven. "I'm ready go ahead," Frank says. "Anytime, now."

Steven looks over at Azreal and waits for him to respond like a jester waiting for his king's command.

"Like I said," Azreal says, "the list was complete, but we will check on our end. I'm sure it was probably a mistake on your end. Gentleman, if there is nothing else, that will conclude our meeting."

Azreal pushes a button on the phone that is in front of him and rings the receptionist. It takes a moment, but she answers with the typical response, "Yes sir."

"Our meeting is over," Azreal says into the phone intercom, "if you could, come and see these gentlemen out."

Azreal hangs up the phone as Gabriel stands up and walks to the large conference room doors.

"This way, gentleman," Gabriel says and opens one of the large doors with ease.

“You two can wait in front of the elevator,” Gabriel says and points down the hallway.

Dan starts to neatly put all his papers back in the brown folder, in the same order that he removed them. He stands to leave, and Frank follows close behind Dan. Gabriel glances them both up and down as they walk from the conference room. Dan returns the hard look at Gabriel as he passes him on the way out of the room.

“See, I told you we weren’t going to get the truth from these guys,” Dan says to Frank as they walk down the hall, but loud enough for the others in the conference room to hear.

Gabriel shuts the door hard behind them. They both glance back as the heavy door shuts, leaving them alone in the hallway.

Gabriel quickly spins around and walks back to the table, then slams his hands on the table surface. The table shakes, and the others remove their hands from it. He leans forward, staring back and forth at Azreal and Haley.

“I told you three that we shouldn’t have started this back up!” Gabriel says.

Azreal looks over at Steven, “Steven, leave the room, please.”

Steven grabs up the papers in front of him then practically runs out of the room.

"Samuel, I have gone along with this for too many years, now!" Gabriel shouts. "I know this is your last wish to give the humans one more drug and to settle our affairs with your friends, but haven't we helped them enough to clear your consciences by now?"

"They have the compound list and samples," Haley says. "Do you think they could figure it out?"

"You fool, they aren't going to figure it out; they are going to figure us out!" Gabriel says as he slams his right hand back on the table again.

Azreal stands up and walks away from the table, "Both of you, calm down. They aren't going to figure anything out. We still have a lot of friends that never want any of this coming to light. We will keep moving forward and reconnect with some old friends. Now, is a perfect time."

"You sure those friends haven't got in car wrecks, also!" Gabriel snaps.

"We can't just stop helping them," Samuel says with a slow soft voice. "We all know that this is the last time that I am able to help and soon, I will be gone. You must all do what is best for each of you and our group. It's been thirty-eight years since we discovered what we are really capable of, and none of us wants to go back to the life we were forced to live before."

"Speak for yourself, Samuel," Gabriel says with his voice teasing. "The old days weren't that bad for me; my conscience is fine."

* * *

CHAPTER TWO

The Year Is 1980

Emma, an elderly and frail looking lady, is laying in a hospital bed. Through a window in the room, one can see that the outside world is dark, and the night sky is covered with ominous clouds that look ready to start dropping rain on the city at any time. Sitting in a chair next to her bed is a much younger looking Samuel, holding Emma's hand tightly.

The sound of the hospital machines beep in repetitions and there is a coldness hanging in the air, it's the coldness associated with most hospitals. An older male doctor wearing glasses and a stethoscope draped around his neck walks into the room holding Emma's chart under his arm. "Hello Emma, how are you feeling tonight?"

"I feel fine," Emma says, "is that good news you have on that chart?"

"Well, we have several things we need to discuss," the doctor says. "It's probably better if we talk in private, are you two friends? related? I haven't seen you here for any of Emma's appointments before?"

"This is Samuel," Emma explains, "he is a very old and personal friend of mine, but he has commitments during the daytime and couldn't make it to any of those appointments. It's fine for us to talk about anything in front of him."

The Doctor pulls a chair over to the bed and sits on it, "Well, Emma, you know, we have been running tests and weighing our options now for a while. I was hopeful that the chemotherapy would have a positive effect on the cancer and hopefully put it in remission or maybe slow it down, but it doesn't look like we were able to do that."

Samuel interrupts with a crackle in his voice. "So, she is going to have to do the chemo again?"

Emma looks over at Samuel with sad, old eyes, "No, Samuel. That's not what the doctor is saying."

"I'm afraid Emma is right," the doctor says. "At this point, we have done all that modern medicine can do. This is a very aggressive form of cancer that we just didn't catch early enough."

Samuel lets go of Emma's hand and stands up, then turns around and walks a few feet from her bed looking away from her and the Doctor, just staring at the blank white wall in the room.

"Emma, would you like me to come back in a little while to talk about your options?" The doctor asks.

"No, Samuel will be fine," Emma says, "we have talked about this possibility and he understands, go ahead please doctor."

"The best thing to do now is go home and enjoy the time you have with your family and friends and be as comfortable as you can. I can prescribe several different medications to help you with that," The doctor stands and pushes his chair back against the wall. "I'll leave you two to talk and come back a little later to check on you again."

"Thank you, doctor," Emma says and flickers her eyes that are now starting to fill with tears.

The Doctor picks up his clipboard and then rubs Emma's arm softly before leaving the room and closing the door behind him. A stillness and sorrow are left behind clinging to the air. Samuel turns and walks back to Emma's bed, then practically collapses to one knee. He takes Emma's hand in both of his, clinching it tightly. Emma gazes at him and a single tear rolls slowly down her cheek.

"I can't let you go!" Samuel says while trying to hold back tears that he wished he was able to cry. "You are my soulmate! It has taken lifetimes to find you. You know, this doesn't have to be the end! You know we can live on forever together."

"We are Soulmates, and we always will be, my love," Emma says and moves her other hand up to rub Samuel's cool cheek. "We have talked about this, and you know, I could never be like you. We have had a great life together for the last thirty years. It's my time, and I'm okay. Let me go, my love. Let me go."

Samuel weakly buries his face in her bedside, while Emma rubs the back of his head. They sit in the room listening only to the rhythmic beats of the hospital machines.

* * *

A few days later, Emma lays in the comfort of her bed at her and Samuel's large country house, located on the sprawling compound around Old World Pharmaceuticals. She looks tired and frailer than before. The color is almost completely gone form her once bright cheeks and endless smile, the end is near. There are other people in the room, family and friends. Azreal, Gabriel, Haley and Samuel are standing on one side of the room.

"I need to talk to you," Samuel whispers in a low voice to Azreal, and Gabriel. "It concerns us all."

Samuel walks out of the bedroom and Azreal, Gabriel and Haley follow. They walk from the room down a hallway and into the living room. The room is an open plan large living room and other people fill the space milling around, talking to each other and snacking from a table filled with food and drinks.

A six-year-old girl, Angela Thomson, a small child bored from being in a group of adults all day and full of energy is playing with a ball when Azreal, Gabriel, Haley and Samuel pass through the room. Angela bounces the ball at Azreal as he is walking by. Azreal catches the ball quickly, then notices the small girl who bounced it at him. Angela's eyes are big and innocent looking back at him. Azreal stops and then walks over to the child to kneel down to put them face to face. Angela's bright eyes stare at him as he hands the ball back to her.

"You caught the ball, so now, we are friends," Angela says with the biggest smile she can make.

"We are?" Azreal asks trying to return the big smile.

"Yes, we are!" Angela says. "Do you want to play with me?"

Angela's mother, Lisa Thomson walks over to young Angela and Azreal. Azreal stands to face her.

"I am so sorry," Lisa says. "Angela, leave this nice man alone."

"It's okay," Azreal replies to Lisa and then looks back at Angela and says. "I was just talking about playing ball with my new friend, but I have a few things I need to take care of first. Then, we will play." Azreal rubs the top of the small girl's head before he turns and walks over to join Gabriel, Haley and Samuel, who have been waiting for him at the beginning of another hallway leading away from the living room.

Azreal turns back and says to Angela "I will see you in a little bit, my new friend," Angela smiles from ear to ear.

"Okay, I'm Angela," she yells back across the room.

"It's nice to meet you, Angela," Azreal shouts back as he walks down the hallway with the others.

The group enters a two-story library room filled from wall to wall with books and artwork, separating the rows of books. In the corner of the room are a massive fireplace and a scrolling circularly shaped staircase leading to the second-floor catwalk that circles the room with even more row upon row of books, most in shelves but some staked up on the floor also. Samuel closes the door behind them, then walks over to a desk and flicks on a desk light to add more visibility to the dimly lit room. He sits on a large couch in the middle of the room and bends over to put his face in his hands, again wishing tears could flow out of him, but no tears come. Then gathers himself and straightens up to look at the group.

"I have lived for a very, very long time," Samuel says. "Emma has become the only thing that is worth continuing on for, but now..."

Azreal puts his hand on Samuel's shoulder to comfort him.

"Why have you not turned her?" Gabriel asks.

"Killing is easy for you, Gabriel!" Samuel says back at him. "You have always enjoyed it!"

"But we don't kill anymore, even though we could rule this world!" Gabriel says. "The only thing we kill now are animals, just like all the humans do. Those are the rules now, right? Correct me if I am wrong."

Gabriel turns his back on them and walks a few feet away, throwing his hands in the air. Azreal rolls his eyes at him and then focuses back on Samuel.

"So, what are you telling us, Samuel?" Azreal asks.

“That I’m done with this life,” Samuel says. “I have no reason to keep living. I am going to go with Emma when it’s her time.”

“Why have you not turned her?” Gabriel spinning around to look back at Samuel and asks with disgust. “Would you like me to do it for you?”

“Because our life isn’t for her!” Samuel says. “She doesn’t want it! Can’t you understand that?”

“Gabriel, this is Samuel’s decision, not yours!” Azreal snaps at him.

Samuel bends down and puts his face back into both of his hands again. Gabriel walks back toward them glaring hard at Azreal.

As Gabriel approaches, he says “You’re right, Azreal, this is Samuel’s decision and It looks like he has made his choice.” Gabriel reaches down and gently lifts Samuel’s head up, at the same time as he kneels down on one knee, so they are looking at each other, face-to-face. Azreal lets go of Samuel’s shoulder and takes a step back.

“Emma is an old, sick human who probably isn’t thinking straight,” Gabriel says. “I don’t think you want to die yet my friend, but if you go that way, and you want to see whatever is waiting for us after this world, you should go together with your love Emma. That means you could turn her, and then, if you both still want to go, then walk into the sun together as it should be!"

Gabriel lets go of Samuel's chin and stands back up, turns his back and walks a few feet away from him.

Samuels mind begins racing as he thinks about what Gabriel said. "Maybe she will change her mind, and you can go back to your happy little life with her," Gabriel says with his back still turned away from Samuel and the others.

Gabriel opens the door and exits the room as Samuel looks up at Azreal with hope in his eyes.

* * *

CHAPTER THREE

The Year Is 2018

The compounding lab at Old World Pharmaceuticals is filled with science equipment and computers. Jacob Ellis, a young lab technician is eagerly looking at test results that he has just pulled off a printer and placed on a clipboard to review. Steven O'Hara enters the lab and walks over to Jacob.

Jacob stops reading the papers and looks up at Steven. "Hi, I'm Jacob, I was told that you are in charge of, well pretty much everything in the lab?" Jacob says as he sits the clipboard down to shake hands with Steven.

"Yes, I am responsible to account to the owners for all our work. Sorry, we haven't had a chance to meet sooner," Steven says. "I know you have been here, what, at least a week? I saw your job application when you were being considered for this job and wanted to meet you sooner."

"When I applied to work here, I heard it was a great company, that without question, has done great things with their new drug development programs," Jacob says. "But this work schedule is a little crazy, right?"

"I'm not sure I am following you?" Steven says with a confused look on his face.

"Don't get me wrong," Jacob says, "so far, this looks like a great place to work, the pay and benefits can't be beaten, but why is the building almost completely closed during the day and all the work shifts are at night?" Steven pats Jacob on the shoulder a few times.

"Look at it this way, you're one of the lucky ones," Steven says, "if you have something to do during the day now you have time to do it, isn't that great. Now, let's get back to work, so we can get those latest test results ready. I know management is looking forward to seeing them. It was nice meeting you, Jacob, I'm sure you will enjoy working here."

Steven looks down at a clipboard he had been holding under his arm as he walks away. Jacob goes back to work in front of some computer testing equipment and begins to take notes on his clipboard. He continues his work making time pass without noticing. A clock on the wall spins fast from 10:15 pm to 3:00 am.

Jacob is sitting at his desk in the corner of the science lab looking at a report and making notes on it when Azreal walks in the room and over to Jacob. Azreal observes the young man hard at work and says, "Good evening, Jacob, how is your report coming along on the compounding process for substances eight through ten?"

Steven walks over to Jacob's desk and stands next to Azreal waiting for his response.

"The report is almost done sir," Jacob says, "but to get the full picture of how the substances will all work together, it's helpful to know what substances we are working with. Substance thirteen is just listed as a trade secret? It's also not listed in the original proposal for this drug? Is it just missing? Maybe an oversight?"

"You were asked to run a compounding test on eight through ten, not thirteen," Azreal says as he crosses his arms in front of him. "I know you want to be as helpful as possible with getting this new medication to the market where it can help save thousands, if not millions of people. But for that to happen we all have a part to play, and you know what your part is now, eight through ten."

"Yes, sir," Jacob says. "I'll get back on that and have my report to you in the afternoon, I mean, this morning. Sorry, just adjusting to the night shifts."

"Go ahead and just turn that into Steven, so he can check your work," Azreal says, as he uncrosses his arms and walks away from Jacob's desk, then out a door into a hallway. Steven eyes Jacob for a moment before returning to his own work area.

Hours later, Azreal and Steven stand in the hallway outside of the compounding lab, looking at Jacob through a glass window that lines the entire compounding lab.

"Did we make a mistake, hiring this one?" Azreal asks while rubbing his chin. "He is smart but maybe a little too inquisitive for his own good. We just don't need that with this last drug."

"No sir, he is just young and wants to impress," Steven says. "I'll keep him in line, you don't need to worry."

"So, how did he get access to the complete list?" Azreal asks. "Thirteen shouldn't have been anywhere on his list."

"It's my fault," Steven says. "I must have run my list, instead of the employee list, when I gave him the compounding assignment. I'm sorry sir it won't happen again."

"Let's hope not," Azreal says, "for his sake."

Azreal turns and walks away from Steven down a long hallway. Steven walks back into the compounding lab and straight over to Jacob who is sitting at his desk.

"You know, Jacob," Steven says as he rests his hands on the desk to lean closer to Jacob, "I want to see you do good here. It's much safer for you if you talk to Azreal as little as possible. You should also avoid talking to Gabriel as much as you can."

"Safer?" Jacob asks.

"History is going to remember these men as some of the greatest of all time, I just want you to be part of that, Okay?" Steven says. "You understand?"

"Yes, sir," Jacob says. "I understand."

* * *

Frank and several other FDA agents sit at an oval conference table in the FDA building, across from them sit two FBI agents. Shane Armstrong, early 30s, eager for the next big arrest and Mike Brown, a mid-40s man that covered his balding head with an FBI hat. Mike definitely had the look of a cop, all business and a hard look, twenty years of being a cop had taken a toll on him. The rest of the office is the typical low budget government furnishing you would expect to see. Dan is standing at the head of the table, in front of a cork-board that's next to a chalkboard ready and eager to give his presentation to the group.

"OWP" is written at the top of the board. Lines in the red thread linking "Azreal", "Haley", "Samuel", and "Gabriel" to "OWP". Under their names are various names of drugs and the years they went on the market. Angela Thomson now in her late 30s, she is no longer the little girl that bounced a ball at Azreal so many years ago. Walks in and sits down at the far end of the table.

"Thank you for joining us," Dan says. "For those of you who don't know, this is our new Field Office Director Angela Thompson."

Angela sits down and looks around the room at the other agents. They all make kind gestures towards her and she returns the favor. "It looks like we have another agency with us today."

"I felt it was important to bring in the FBI, also, due to this being such a large company and we're crossing state lines," Dan says.

"Let's get going, Dan," Angela says. "I have other things on my schedule today."

Dan wastes no time, turning to point at the cork-board and starts the briefing.

"We are all familiar with Old World Pharmaceuticals," Dan says, "they are without a doubt the most successful drug company in the world. They've been in business for about thirty-five years now. This company burst on the scene back in 1985, when they discovered a cure for Ebola, and, out of the kindness of their hearts, they didn't charge anyone for that drug well anyone except all of us. The U.S. government picked up the tab for that, making these guys very, very wealthy almost overnight."

"Wait a minute, are we talking about the cancer company here?" Shane asks. "The one that has almost got rid of it?"

"Almost! Almost? Far from it," Dan says, "there are still a lot of people dying from it every day."

Mike puts his hand on Shane's arm gently pulling him back some to get his attention.

"We know about this company," Mike says, "We have run across them several times over the years for different reasons."

"Well, all you hear is good things about them helping people in the news," Shane says with a shrug.

"Mike, where did you get this guy?" Dan says while looking at Shane. "Are you on this team or there team?"

"Dan, get back to the briefing," Angela says.

Dan shakes off his stare at Shane and continues with "Next, in the late 1980s, they released three different types of drugs, all of them treated cancers, mainly in adolescents." Dan takes out a packet of pictures from a stack of papers in front of him on the table and passes the pictures around the table.

The photograph is of Azreal, Haley, and Samuel in the 1980s. Standing together with blank expressionless looks on each of their faces.

"Next on the list, in the early 1990s, they develop a cure for leukemia," Dan says. "This made them all billionaires. That's with a B, not an M."

The picture of Azreal has now made its way to around the table to Angela, who can't stop looking at it. Locked onto the picture long enough for everyone at the table to notice her.

"Angela, are you okay?" Frank asks. "Do you know any of them?"

"Everyone in the world knows their names," Angela says. "Azreal just looks so familiar. I'm sure I've just seen him on TV or something. Go ahead and continue, Dan."

"Here is the kicker, the Ebola drug was formulated here in the U.S. but manufactured in Africa and distributed by our military," Dan says. "Then, the drug and all its records get locked up, and no one is allowed to see any of that research."

"So, when did our department sign off on that?" Frank asks.

"We didn't," Dan says. "We also didn't sign off on the three other cancer drugs, because that research was connected with the Ebola research. In the interest of national security, I guess the FDA doesn't need to know what these guys are doing."

"So, you're saying this company isn't even going through the FDA?" Shane asks. "How is that possible? I thought that was your guy's job?"

"Bingo, now you're catching up," Dan says to Shane. "It's been ten years since they have done anything new but now, they're back, why? Why start doing new drugs now? When I went back and started looking at their older drugs in the databases, I couldn't find any of the normal stuff you would find with any of the clinical testings. It's like none of it was done. And the stuff I did find either got the fuck redacted out of it or was just missing. And we have a bunch of these forms."

Dan takes a stack of papers that all look the same and hands them out to everyone at the table. On the papers in different spots, it read in bold, underlined lettering, "Redacted by the U.S. Government. NOT FOR PUBLIC VIEWING."

"I have Frank working on getting the originals from the archives in D.C," Dan says.

"This is in our records?" Angela asks. "We are the Government!"

"When Dan asked me to check on what we have on the company, I ran into similar omissions in our data," Mike says. "I also couldn't really find any personal information on any of the principles for this business dating to prior to them being in business. It's kind of odd, to say the least."

"I don't like what I've heard here, but I also haven't heard anything that would be considered criminal," Angela says. "Bad record keeping on our end? Dan, unless you have something else, I think we are done here."

"Angela, I know something is wrong here!" Dan says. "Really wrong!"

"Well, then bring me something else, but we aren't wasting any more time on a witch hunt!" Angela says. "That's not how we operate.

I know you requested to work on this case, and I did you a favor by giving it to you, but if your personal judgments get in the way, I will remove you." Angela says and then gets up to leave the room.

"I'll keep looking and if I find anything, I'll let you know," Mike says. "Not sure what I could find but what the hell."

* * *

Azreal is at his desk, looking over papers and logbooks. Even though its night outside, he has the shutters closed over his windows. Haley walks in and leans against a wall waiting for him to look up at her. "You wanted to see me?" she asks.

"Yes, I was in the main lab yesterday, picking up the compounding results on eight through ten from our new hire, Jacob, and he asked about substance thirteen," Azreal says after looking up from his papers at her.

Before Haley can answer, Samuel and Gabriel, walk into Azreal's office and sit down in chairs against the wall.

"Who is Jacob, and why would he have access to thirteen?" Haley asks. "There should be no record of that anywhere other than with us."

"Yes, with us, and Steven," Azreal says. "I talked to Steven about being more careful, but you might want to check to make sure Jacob is the only one who saw this."

"We all know this couldn't go on forever," Samuel says. "The work we have done has helped millions of humans, but it's time you all start to think about an end game."

"What end game is that Samuel?" Gabriel smirks. "The one that you and Emma have chosen? No, thanks!"

"That's not what I meant," Samuel replies.

"You two didn't know your director friend at the FDA was gone?" Gabriel asks. "Is that one of those loose ends you told me not to worry about?"

"No, Gabriel," Haley says, "we didn't know he was gone, but there is nothing to worry about here. This drug will go through, just like all the others did."

"So, do you still have your political friends?" Gabriel asks. "Have you even checked to see if they're still alive? Or have we outlived them too?"

Samuel gets up and starts to walk to the door, then stops to say. "I am going home to spend what time I have left with Emma, Gabriel, there is no need for this conversation; we all know this is the last time we can help the humans."

"Samuel, I love you, and I respect your decisions, but I will never make the same trade you made for your immortality," Gabriel says.

Samuel puts his hand on Gabriel's shoulder for an instant, then turns and walks out of the room.

"If you three aren't careful, that agent is going to find out what compound thirteen is, and then, what will you do?" Gabriel asks.

Gabriel stands and leaves the room. Haley sits down in a chair on the other side of Azreal's desk and reaches over to pick up Angela Thompson's business card from the desk.

"After all these years, why did you not know she had become the director?" Haley asks.

Azreal stands and walks to the window and opens the blinds to looks out into the darkness, gazing at the far-off lights of Huston. "It was better for her and me that I stop keeping track of her" Azreal replies.

* * *

CHAPTER FOUR

The Year Is 1980

Samuel, Azreal, Gabriel, and Haley, along with Emma's family and friends, stand around talking inside of Samuel and Emma's living room. A nurse comes into the room nervously looking for Samuel. The nurse walks up to Samuel and whispers in his ear. Samuel lowers his head for a second then looks back up and over at Azreal, before turning and walking toward the master bedroom, Azreal, Haley and Gabriel quickly follow behind him.

Emma is in bed, unconscious. Several of her friends are in the room. Samuel, Gabriel, Haley, and Azreal enter the room. Azreal turns to stop the nurse from entering the room as Samuel walks over to Emma and kneels beside her, taking her hand in both of his.

"Thank you for all that you have done, but your services will no longer be needed," Azreal says to the nurse in a low voice. Haley and Gabriel inconspicuously approach the rest of the people in the room, one by one, whispering to them. Slowly the room empties out. Azreal shuts the door to the room and locks it as the last person leaves.

"Emma, I know we have talked, but..." Samuel says with a crackle to his voice. "I know what you want, but it wasn't really you telling me that. You have been sick. I know you love me and want to continue with me, I know it. So...so, this way we can still be together, and if it isn't what you want, I promise you we will end it together, how it should be." Samuel slowly stands and leans over Emma. With his fingers, he gently rubs the side of her colorless cheek, and then over her pale lips.

"Samuel, it's time," Gabriel says. "You need to do it now, or she will be gone."

Samuel looks over at Gabriel, then lifts his forearm up to his mouth. Large, sharp fangs grow from his teeth. He bites deep into his forearm, and blood starts to slowly flow from his arm. Samuel looks up at the ceiling as he lowers his arm to right above Emma's mouth. A few drops of blood fall onto her lips and chin.

"I am sorry, please forgive me" Samuel whispers as his blood starts to enter Emma's mouth.

From a bathroom connected to the master bedroom emerges the six-year-old Angela Thompson.

"What are you doing to her?" Angela asks.

Samuel surprised by the child's voice, quickly jerks his arm away from Emma's mouth and stops the blood from dropping onto her lips. Gabriel is standing closest to Angela. In an instant, his sharp fangs snap out, and he turns and lunges at the child. Faster than light, Azreal already has the child in his arms, protecting her, with his back to Gabriel. Gabriel lands on top of Azreal's back, clinking him with strong hands and digging sharp fingernails into Azreal's arms and shoulders to hold on to him. With a quick, powerful spin Azreal throws Gabriel to the floor. Haley wastes no time and leaps on top of Gabriel, holding him down.

"Azreal, you cannot let her go!" Gabriel hisses while trying to free himself from Haley who is still holding him down. "She has seen us for what we are!"

Azreal pulls the shaking and terrified child away from his chest and looks deep into her eyes.

"Sleep... Sleep... Sleep," Azreal says.

The young Angela slowly fades into unconsciousness. Her small head slumps over Azreal's shoulder. Azreal turns back to glare at Gabriel.

"I place this girl under my protection," Azreal says. "I will be responsible for her and all her actions from now on. Gabriel, you will not harm her!"

Azreal unlocks the look and walks out of the room. Haley quickly lets go of Gabriel and moves to the door to lock it again. Samuel is now sitting on the floor, next to Emma's bed. Emma is lifeless laying in the bed. Samuel's head is buried in his hands whimpering.

"What have I done?" Samuel asks. "I shouldn't have done this… I know what she wanted… This is not what she wanted…" Samuel continues to mumble to himself.

Azreal, holding the sleeping Angela, walks into Samuel and Emma's dining room and up to Angela's mother, Lisa.

"It looks like it's been a long day for this little one," Azreal hands Angela to Lisa.

"Awww, thank you," Lisa says as she takes the sleeping child from Azreal. "Yeah, I'm sure she is ready to go home and go to bed. There's not much more we can do here tonight."

"Yes, I think it's better for everyone to leave now," Azreal says. "It's getting late."

Azreal softly rubs the little girl's head while smiling at her.

“I’m sure she will want to sleep in tomorrow, it’s been a long day, so go easy on her,” Azreal says to Lisa. And then turns to leaves the dining room to make his way back to Emma’s room.

There is a knock on the door. Haley quickly opens the door, and Azreal walks in. Haley puts her hand on Azreal’s shoulder. They both look over to see Samuel, sitting on the bed with Emma.

Emma is sitting up, fully awake and alert, brushing her hair that is slowly returning to its natural brown color. Her complexion has the color of a healthy and much younger woman. The pale coldness that was in her face is all but gone now.

“What happened to her?” Azreal asks, hardly believing his eyes. “How is this possible?”

“We have no idea,” Haley says.

Gabriel now looking at Emma more closely says “Clearly, the turning process has several different levels we were unaware of.”

“None of us has ever stopped in the middle of the turning,” Haley says. “Azreal, have you ever heard of anything from your maker about anything like this?”

“No, nothing... It’s amazing...” Azreal says.

Emma is still brushing her hair and looking around at the others. "It was your blood, right?" Emma asks Samuel. "How much did I have?"

"A drop, maybe less," Samuel says. "I think."

"Well I can tell you a drop will make you feel twenty years younger," Emma exclaims. "Can I have a mirror please." Haley walks to the bathroom and gets a mirror that she hands to Emma.

"I am going to guess your cancer free now also," Azreal says.

Emma looks in the mirror and then looks over at Azreal with a big smile.

"What does this mean?" Haley asks.

"It means that if Emma tests cancer free, we are no longer the enemy of the humans," Azreal says.

"We have something that can help them," Samuel says as he smiles and rubs Emma's shoulder.

"It also means that we have something that they may want to take from us, maybe by force," Gabriel says.

"We also have something that we could sell," Haley says, with a smile.

Gabriel smiles back wickedly at Haley.

"It looks like life just changed for us," Gabriel chuckles.

* * *

CHAPTER FIVE

The Year Is 2018

Dan, Frank and FDA Agent Troy Hanson are in Dan's office setting around his desk that is cluttered with papers they are looking over with names and addresses of Old World Pharmaceutical's employees. Frank closes the shutters a little to block the sunlight and so everyone could see the paperwork more easily. The cluttered desk is clearly making Dan's OCD flare up as he keeps trying to organize the papers as they all shuffle through them.

"This is the newest list you could come up with?" Dan asks frustrated. "These guys have been there forever, they're not going to talk to us."

"Yeah this is it," Frank says and scratches at his head.

"I know they haven't put out anything new in years, but everyone on this list is my dad's age or older," Dan says. "Why are these people even still working, they should be retired somewhere."

"Most of the people on that list aren't working there anymore," Frank says and points at the list.

"Those dates at the end are the last dates they got paid from Old World," Frank says.

"What about this guy?" Troy asks. "His hire date in only a few weeks ago."

"I guess, they finally ran out of employees and had to finally replace one," Dan says.

Dan looks at the name, then shuffles through some folders on the desk. He matches the name with a folder, then hands the folder to Frank.

"Look for an address in there," Dan says while Frank flips through the file.

"Bingo, I got it," Frank says.

"It looks like we will be paying Jacob a visit real soon," Dan says. "Real soon boys."

Troy and Frank leave Dan's office and are walking down a hallway to their own offices. Most of the officers' doors are closed as they walk by them.

"I'm all about doing my job, but since this Old World case got going, Dan has had a hard-on for these guys," Frank says.

"Can you blame him?" Troy replies.

"What do you mean?" Frank asks.

"He is never going to accept what happened," Troy says.

"Maybe, I'm missing something here," Frank says. "What happened?"

"Fucking new guy, it was before your time," Troy says.

Troy stops at his office and motions Frank to come in. He pushes the door open and flicks the light on, though it does little in the sunlight. Troy sits at his desk and Frank takes a seat across from him.

"Shut the door, fucking new guy, and I'll enlighten you," Troy says.

Frank gets back up and shuts the door, then looks back to Tory with anticipation.

"You know, this doesn't leave this room, right?" Troy says. "I don't want to be the guy that brings up old shit, plus I really don't want to get on Dan's bad side."

“I may be new here, but I’m not a fucking new guy,” Frank says. “Come on spill it.”

“Okay, okay,” Troy says. “You see that pic of Dan and his daughter on his desk?”

“Yeah, I’ve seen it,” Frank says while he imagines the picture in his head. “Old pic, I’m pretty sure he looks my age in it.”

“Look at you, investigator,” Troy says. “That’s right, it’s an old pic, but he doesn’t have a daughter anymore.”

“What the fuck?” Frank asks.

“Dan’s daughter had cancer,” Troy explains, “and she might have made it, but even with him pulling strings here to get on the list for the right doctors that had access to the drugs from Old World, they still only made small batches.”

“What the fuck?” Frank says again. “So, she didn’t get the meds that she needed?”

Troy picks up a pen on his desk and throws it at Frank.

“You’re back to being the fucking idiot,” Troy says. “I told you he doesn’t have a daughter anymore. So, is it Old Worlds fault? I don’t know, but I do know Dan thinks it is and he’s holding a grudge against them that isn't ever going to go away. I don't think he'll stop at anything until he finds his answers."

"Wow," Frank says.

* * *

CHAPTER SIX

The Year Is 2018

Gabriel sits at his desk, working on his computer. Samantha walks in and shuts the door behind her. She sits on the edge of Gabriel's desktop so close to his keyboard, that it's impossible for him to work on it.

"How did your meeting with the FDA guys go?" Samantha asks.

Gabriel leans back in his chair and places his hand on Samantha's calf, slowly rubbing it. She doesn't object.

"My relationship with Azreal is old, and it is hard for me to imagine life without him, but it might be time for us to part ways soon if they continue with this new drug," Gabriel says.

"What about Haley and Samuel?" Samantha asks.

"We all know what's going to happen to Samuel, probably very soon," Gabriel says. "Haley will go where ever Azreal goes. All I can say for sure is that our future is what we make of it."

"Well, I hope our future is more like our past!" Samantha growls.

Gabriel and Samantha both look at each other and laugh. Gabriel gets up and walks to the office window to look out at the lights, far off in the distance.

"So, what are we doing this weekend?" Samantha asks. "More of the same? Say yes!"

"That is definitely a bad idea, now that we have our new FDA problems," Gabriel says. "A guy named Dan."

Samantha gets up and walks over to Gabriel and rubs his shoulders. "Hasn't it been fun, though?" Samantha asks. "Like old times again. The thrill of the hunt."

"I didn't say it hasn't been fun," Gabriel says. "I just said it was a bad idea for now."

"So, blame me," Samantha says. "I always make bad decisions."

"We need to be even more careful now, with this FDA guy looking around," Gabriel says. "He seems to be the type that is going to cause problems."

"That's my boy," Samantha says. "I'll be at your house Saturday night."

Samantha slaps Gabriel on his ass as she walks to the door.

"Hey, I didn't say we were doing anything this weekend!" Gabriel says.

"But you didn't say we weren't doing anything either," Samantha says with a grin from ear to ear.

* * *

The scientists in the lab are wrapping up their work for the night, shutting down machines and turning off computers. Steven is looking at more test results with Jacob behind his cluttered desk. Haley pushes the door to the lab open and walks straight over to Steven and Jacob.

"It's almost quitting time," Haley says.

"Yeah, we are just finishing up reviewing the results of the last of the tests before we can start our first compounding of XP1," Steven says. "Just a few more tests, and we'll be ready, it's really exciting."

"Good job, Steven," Haley says. "Let's keep this moving along. We need to get those samples soon. We should probably talk about that later, see me in my office before you leave tonight."

Haley turns to walk away, but Jacob is now standing behind Haley, between her and the exit door for the lab.

"Excuse me, Ma'am," Jacob says. "I have a few questions for you."

Haley walks around Jacob and toward the door pretending not to hear the young scientist. As Haley approaches the exit door to the lab, she turns to look over her shoulder and back at Jacob with a cold glance and says, "You can talk to Steven about any questions you have." The automatically opening door opens and shuts behind her as she leaves the room.

"What are you doing?" an irritated Steven asks. "I told you not to talk to any of the owners unless they have questions for you!"

"I'm sorry, sir," Jacob says. "I know you helped get me hired here, but these test results just don't seem right to me. It's just, that I feel something odd is going on with this new medicine." Jacob holds the pad of paper he is holding up to show Steven.

Steven looks around to see if anyone else is nearby. Most of the people that had been working in the lab have already left for the night, but there are still a few lab technicians rapping their areas up. Steven grabs Jacob firmly by his arm and pulls him behind some lab equipment.

"Look, Jacob," Steven says. "I like you, and I want to see you do good here at Old World, but you have to listen to me when I tell you to stop making waves. Just do your job and everything will be fine. I just don't want to see anything happen to you."

"What would happen to me?" Jacob asks. "I'm just trying to do my job and there is a certain level of ethics that I would like to maintain."

Steven clearly frustrated with Jacob says sharply, "Wrap up here, go home, and think about what I told you." Steven goes back to his area in the lab to organize the lab test papers while Jacob cleans up his station and packs it up for the next day. Steven glances over at Jacob as he leaves the lab.

Haley is sitting at her desk in her office looking at her computer and Azreal is standing next to her looking at the same computer screen, when Steven knocks on the open door to Haley's office. "Come in Steven."

"You wanted to see me," Steven says. "Is this a bad time?"

"No, Steven," Haley says. "Come in and have a seat." Steven walks in and sits down, only halfway shutting the office door behind him.

Azreal stops looking at the computer screen and walks over to a chair that is against the adjacent wall and sits down.

The final lab employees are leaving the building for the weekend. Jacob sees Steven walk into Haley's office, unseen by Steven, Jacob follows him, but stops just outside of Haley's office and leans against the wall, eavesdropping on the conversation happening in the office.

"Your new hire, Jacob, is a little too curious for his own good," Haley says.

"Yes, I have noticed that also," Steven says. "I have talked to him a few times now about focusing more on his work and leaving the business part to management."

"With our new FDA problems, we can't have anything slipping out," Haley says. "You need to get rid of him before the problem develops into something more serious that might require us to take care of ourselves, you understand what I mean Steven."

"He is a good kid and I don't want to see anything bad happen to him, so I'll make sure he understands his place here or I'll fire him before you need to become part of it," Steven reassures them.

"It sounds like you like him?" Azreal asks. "Let's wait on getting rid of him for now, we just need everything to stay moving along without any new problems."

"I'll keep a closer eye on him," Steven says with a slight gulp of the throat. "Thank you, Azreal."

"We have been reviewing your work and it looks like the first samples are ready to be mixed," Haley says. "Are you staying this weekend in the basement lab to get them ready?"

"Yes, I was planning on being here all weekend to get that done," Steven says.

"Okay, I will check back in on you this weekend to see how they are going," Azreal says.

"If you don't mind me asking why the rush with this new drug?" Steven says. "Wouldn't it be better to back off some, maybe take it slow until we have everything right, and it's not rushed?"

Azreal and Haley look at each other, and then back to Steven with a little glimmer in both of their eyes.

"Tell him, he has been with us long enough to understand," Azreal says to Haley.

"Tell me what?" Steven asks.

Haley looks back at Steven and says "Okay, we have an old friend that we met around the same time we met you, He helped us get going in the beginning, and now, he is asking for a favor."

“The new drug?” Steven asks.

“Yes, XP1,” Haley says.

“But why not wait and avoid any problems that might happen with rushing it?” Steven asks. “It still needs more testing, not to mention, it hasn’t been approved for production yet.”

“This friend of ours is being,” Haley stops for a moment thinking about what to say next, “well, a little insistent on timely delivery.”

“So, not really a friend anymore?” Steven says, his insides beginning to grow uneasy with the situation.

Azreal stands and walks over to Steven. “You could say that,” Azreal says and places his hand on Steven’s shoulder and looking deep into Steven’s eyes. “You know time is of the essence with this and I know we can trust you to deliver, Steven.”

“You know, I have always done my best for both of you and this company,” Steven replies, unable to look away from Azreal’s stare.

Jacob quickly walks away from Haley’s office door and heads toward the main exit for the building hoping that nobody sees him. He glances over his shoulder nervously to make sure that Jacob hasn’t left the office yet. As he reaches the exit door and pushes through it and outside into the cold morning air. A feeling of relief fills him.

Then as quickly as relief filled him it leaves being replaced with depression and fear as he picks up his pace to a jog toward his car.

* * *

The sun shines through the window and onto Angela Thomson sitting at her desk in the FDA building, she is on the phone and has multiple papers on her desktop in organized piles.

"Just working mom, still getting used to the new job," Angela says into the phone.

"That's good Ang, I just wanted to tell you again how proud I am of you," Lisa Thomson's voice comes through the phone.

"Thank you, Mom," Angela says. "An odd thing happened in a meeting I had. I saw a picture of the owners of a company called Old World Pharmaceuticals. Have you heard of them?"

"Is that the cancer company?" Lisa asks.

"Yeah, that's them," Angela says.

"Yes, Ang I've heard of them, I think the whole world knows about that company," Lisa says.

"One of the owners looked so familiar," Angela says. "When I saw the picture of him, it was more like I knew him personally than just looking at the picture of a stranger."

"Well, Ang, I have no idea what you're working on with that company, but from what I've heard they do really good things," Lisa says with sincerity. "So, I wouldn't waste too much time with them, I'm sure you have more important things to be working on, now that you're the boss."

* * *

A black, four-door sedan pulls up in front of Jacob's house. Dan gets out of the car on the passenger side, holding a thick brown folder. Frank gets out of the driver's side and hurries around the car to catch up with Dan, who is already walking toward the front door of Jacob's house.

"Get a move on, FNG," Dan yells back over his shoulder.

Dan and Frank knock on the front door of Jacob's house. The door opens to Martha Ellis, she has the girl next door look, cute but just average looking for a girl in her early twenty's. Long blonde hair and deep blue eyes. She smiles at the sight of the two men and says, "hello can I help you."

“Hello, I’m Agent Miller with the FDA,” Dan says. “We have a few questions for Jacob Ellis. Is he home?”

“Yeah he is, I think, I’ll check,” Martha says.

“Who are you?” Franks asks.

“I’m Martha, Jacob’s sister,” Martha says and shuts the door.

A few minutes later Jacob opens the door, looking half asleep with messy hair and groggy eyes. He wipes at his face still trying to wake up before looking at the men.

“Sorry, did we catch you at a bad time?” Dan asks. “You sleeping? It’s the middle of the day.”

Jacob looks at Dan with a glare “No, no, not anymore,” Jacob says. “I work nights. Who are you guys again?”

Dan, quick to grab his wallet out of his pocket and flips out the badge hidden inside of it, then with a snap, flips it back shut. Frank slower to get out his badge shows it to Jacob also.

“We are with the FDA,” Dan says.

“I didn’t know the FDA had cops,” Jacobs says with a smile.

"Yeah, it has cops," Dan says glaring back at Jacob now. "You mind if we come in? We have some questions for you about Old World Pharmaceuticals."

Jacob opens the door wider and backs up some, then motions for them to come inside. They enter the house and walk through a cluttered living room and into a kitchen. The three of them sit around a kitchen table. Dan opens his folder and takes some papers out, then neatly places them on the table in front of him, as usual. Dan looks over the papers while he slowly and routinely rolls the fingers of his right hand on the table. Index, middle, ring, pinky finger. Slow gentle thuds on the table, over and over.

"So, you're a pretty smart guy, it looks like you have a few degrees," Dan says. "How did you end up working at Old World?"

"I applied, and they hired me," Jacob says with a smug look on his face. "What's this about?"

Dan breaks away from the papers he is looking at to look up at Jacob and asks "So, do you like it there, Jacob?"

"No, not really, it's night shifts, and who wants to work night shifts?" Jacob says with a slight yawn. "So, again, what's this about?"

"We just think something may not be exactly right over there at Old World," Dan says.

"You mean, like working night shifts?" Jacob asks. "There is still no one there that will give me a straight answer on that, along with anything else I try and ask."

"So, you think there might be some problems, also?" Frank asks.

"Yeah, I would say there are problems," Jacob says. "I'm pretty sure they are going to fire me on Monday and that would be a problem for me!"

Dan and Frank look at each other and grin. Dan's finger rolling speeds up.

"So, what would get you fired in only working a few weeks there?" Dan asks.

"Look, I don't want to get in trouble, but what they are doing over there doesn't seem right to me," Jacob says.

"Okay, Jacob," Dan says, "we are going to need you to not get fired just yet. There are a few things we are going to need you to get from inside Old World."

* * *

CHAPTER SEVEN

The Year Is 1984

Through the darkness of the early night, Azreal and Samuel walk up an oversized walkway that is lined with perfectly manicured shrubs and bushes. The walkway leads to the door of a large estate size two-story red brick house. Azreal reaches up and grabs the steel doorknocker that is bolted to one of the over-sized double doors on the front of the house. A minute after Azreal gives two hard knocks that rattle through the house, one of the doors opens to reveal a man in his early 60's and slightly overweight, Senator Thatch.

"Can I help you, gentleman?" Senator Thatch says.

"I understand your wife is sick," Azreal says.

"How did you know that?" Senator Thatch snaps back at Azreal.

"May we come in to talk more about a proposal we have for you?" Azreal asks.

Some time has passed, and the group is sitting in the living room of Senator Thatch's house. The living room is lined with what looks like very expensive art and beautiful vases sitting on a pillar. The light from a fireplace still burning bright is lighting the room, a chandelier helps fill the rest of the dark spots in the room. Azreal and Samuel are setting on a couch while the Senator sits across from them. Separating them is a long short table with several round stains from coffee and drinks that had been left on the table for too long during hours of discussion that had happened around the table for years. Sitting on the other side of the table is Senator Thatch in a very comfortable over-sized and ware out chair that looks like he has spent many hours in it by the fireplace.

The story Azreal spins for the Senator stretches back a thousand years and is incomprehensible to a normal human. It's a story that to the Senator sounds like a fairytale but is so intriguing that the Senator can't help but listen to every word of it waiting for a fantastic ending like a good book.

At the end of the story, Azreal and Samuel sit quietly looking at the Senator, who begins laughing out loud hysterically and slapping his knees as he doubles over from laughing. Then after a moment the Senator composes himself and sits back up to leans back in his big chair to address them. "So, you must admit, your story seems a little farfetched, right?" Senator Thatch says with a grin.

"Yes, I agree it might seem that way to you, but I assure you all of it is true," Azreal says.

"While I have enjoyed this conversation with you gentlemen," Senator Thatch says. "It's getting late and I think I have heard enough tall tells for this evening."

Samuel reaches in his jacket pocket and pulls out a small glass veil with red, almost black blood in it and holds it up in the flickering light from the fireplace for the Senator to see. The Senator leans forward in his chair looking at the glass veil intensely.

"Senator, with a drop of the blood that is in this veil, you could have your wife back, feeling better than she has felt in twenty years," Samuel says, "and with your help bypassing some government regulations, all of mankind can start a new path."

"I don't know what you two are up to, but there is no way I believe any of this horseshit," Senator Thatch says. "It's time I saw you two out!"

Azreal and Samuel look at each other, and then slowly back at Senator Thatch. Azreal leans forward to stare hard at Senator Thatch.

"You will be a true believer in a minute," Azreal says as he opens his mouth and long, sharp fangs snap out from Azreal's teeth.

Faster than light, Azreal leaps directly over the coffee table and is standing in front of Senator Thatch now looking down at him. Senator Thatch jerks back in his chair startled by the speed that Azreal was able to move in front of him. Samuel springs off the couch and in a flash, he is up the stairs standing at the entrance door to the master bedroom of the house.

Thatch knows his wife is in the master bedroom and panic fills him from his toes to his head, as he sees Samuel standing at the door. With every bit of strength, he has he tries to stand to his feet, but it does him no good. He is no match for Azreal as he wraps his cold powerful hands around Thatch's shoulders forcing him back down in his chair. The chair that was so comfortable just moments ago is now the same as a jail cell with no escape.

"NO!" Senator Thatch shouts as he struggles in vain to free himself from Azreal's powerful grip.

The door to the master bedroom flies open, and Samuel enters the room.

The Senator's wife is sleeping peacefully in the comfort of her bed, she is old and skinny, the color in her face that she once had is all but gone now. The cancer she has fought for so long has made her fragile and weak. Samuel enters the room and shuts the door behind him as he walks over to the bed and kneels down to look at her. The Senator's wife rolls over to see the strange man in her room in a weak and scared voice she says, "who are you?"

"I'm not going to hurt you," Samuel says in a gentle and soothing voice. "I'm going to help you. Would you like that?"

The Senator's Wife slowly nods in approval and gives a slight grunt from the pain caused by the motion of rolling over to face Samuel.

Azreal looks up at the stairs, and then back at Senator Thatch before releasing him from his iron grip. Azreal takes a step backwards, allowing Senator Thatch to get up from the chair. Senator Thatch immediately runs for the stairs climbing them fumbling and stumbling, bouncing off the wall and back to the handrail trying to make it to the top as fast as he can.

Senator Thatch burst into the master bedroom slamming the door open as hard as he can but then stops only a few feet into the room. Samuel is standing next to the bed, holding the Senators wife's hand in his. The Senator's Wife is now sitting up in bed smiling and looking at Samuel and then at back at Thatch. The color is coming back to her face. Azreal walks in the room behind Senator Thatch and places his hand softly on the Senator's shoulder.

"Join your wife, Senator," Samuel says. "We can talk when you are ready. We will be downstairs, waiting."

Samuel softy places the hand of the Senator's wife down on the bed and walks past the senator to leave the room with Azreal. Tears roll down Senator Thatch's face as he stares at his wife.

* * *

CHAPTER EIGHT

The Year Is 2018

It's dark outside of the large county style home that Samuel and Emma live in. Rocking chairs sit on the porch that wraps around the house, gently moving with the cold breeze blowing by them. A much older looking Samuel and Emma are sitting snuggled together on a couch in their living room. Emma is sipping tea and wrapped in a blanket to keep warm. A fire is blazing at one end of the living room.

"We have had a great life together, haven't we?" Samuel asks.

"Yes, we have my love," Emma says.

Samuel reaches over to put his hand on Emma's leg and then turns to look into her eyes.

"Do you have any regrets?" Emma asks.

Emma sets her tea on a coffee table, and then turns to face Samuel, putting her hand on top of his.

"No, my love," Samuel says, "there is nothing I would change."

"You could have let me go and lived forever," Emma says.

Emma reaches out to touch Samuel's cold face with both her hands.

"My love, by helping you," Samuel says. "I learned I could help millions of other people. It will never make up for the horrible things I have done to humans, but it gives me some measure of peace. I know Azreal and Haley feel the same way."

"And Gabriel?" Emma asks.

Samuel puts his head down for a moment then gets up from the couch and walks over to the window with his back turned to Emma. For what seems like forever, he stares out the window at the darkness. "Gabriel will have to make his peace with who he is and the things he has done when he is ready," Samuel says. "I truly don't know what will become of him."

* * *

Dan, Frank, Troy, and Angela are sitting around the FDA conference table. Dan has a stack of papers in front of him again, neatly organized. As usual, he is slowly rolling his fingers on the table- index, ring, middle, and pinky, slow taps on the table, over and over.

"So, just to get everyone up to speed, it looks like we have a confidential informant now inside Old World," Dan says as he picks up a paper from the stack in front of him to read from it. "A Jacob Ellis. Frank and I paid him a visit, and he had some interesting stuff to say about Old World."

"Dan, does anyone outside of this room know you talked to this Jacob guy?" Angela asks. "Or what has been going on with your investigation?"

"No, Angela," Dan says. "I wouldn't go over your head. This investigation has been by the book."

"That's not what I meant, Dan," Angela says. "If you haven't talked to anyone then why did I get a call from D.C. this morning, from someone I didn't even know was in my chain of command, asking a lot of questions about Old World?"

"I have no idea why anyone from D.C. would be checking on this?" Dan asks. "Why would they care?"

"Well, that might explain the stuff I got back from records," Frank says as he scratches his head.

"What are you talking about, fucking new guy?" Dan asks.

"You asked me to pull the hard copies of Old World's past submissions for new drugs," Franks says. "I thought it would be harder to get that stuff because of the twenty-year shelf life on the patents before they expired, and the generic versions of those drugs started getting made."

"Yeah, that's right," Dan says. "So, did you get those submissions?"

"Well, not exactly," Frank opens the folder sitting in front of him and passes a handful of papers to Dan in a neat manner.

Dan sets the papers down on the table and starts looking at them. The slow thuds from his finger rolling get faster and faster as he looks through the papers one by one.

"You going to share this with us, Dan?" Angela asks and tries to get a better look at the papers, but Dan is shuffling through them too quick to see anything written on them.

Dan keeps looking through the papers and then stops rolling his finger to scratch his head. Then, back to rolling his finger but now much harder than before.

"This just doesn't make sense," Dan says. "Frank, this is all you got? Fuck, what is this?"

"That's it," Franks says, "That's all they had."

"Thirty years of making some of the world's bestselling drugs and this shit is all you got?" Dan says.

"Dan, give me those papers right now!" Angela yells as her patience runs out.

Dan passes the papers back to Frank, who hands them to Angela. She has the same confused look on her face as she reads through them.

"Redacted for security reasons?" Angela says. "National Security, Classified?"

Angela keeps reading in disbelief as she scans over several pages full of classified marks. She puts the papers down and glances between the others at the table.

"How is that even possible?" Frank asks. "I thought we were the ones that protected the public?"

"What the fuck is that, Angela?" Dan asks, then stands up and begins to pace near the table.

"This is clearly over both of our pay grades, Dan," Angela says. "We are going to pull back on this case until I get more direction from D.C."

"You can't be serious!" Dan stops pacing to protest and approaches the table. "Come on! We are too close to getting these fuckers!"

"Dan, you heard me!" Angela says. "You are off this case! I know this would be too close to home for you!" Dan instantly starts rolling his fingers so hard and fast the table begins to vibrate.

"What the fuck does that mean Angela?" Dan says, now becoming angry at Angela's remark. "Too close to home?"

Angela stands and walks to the door but turns to look at Dan, "You heard me, Dan. You're done with this for now." She walks out the door leaving Dan rolling his fingers.

Frank nods to Dan with a somber look then stands up and leaves the room with Troy.

* * *

Dan is now sitting at his desk sometime after the meeting, still upset with being told to stop investigating the Old World case by Angela. He picks up his office phone and types in a number then looks down at a piece of paper he is holding.

"Mike, what's going on with that wiretap I asked you to set up for this weekend?" Dan asks into the receiver, and he listens to the response. Then says back into the phone, “Of course, I have the warrant; it’s right here in my hand, everything is good to go. You going to get this done for me, or what?”

Dan looks back down at the warrant in his hand. The space for a judge to sign the document is clearly blank. Dan pulls the phone base over to the middle of his desk, so the phone cord will reach as he slides his chair over and inserts the warrant into the paper shredder next to his desk.

“What the fuck, buddy?” Dan says into the phone. “You think I would ask you to do this if the judge hadn’t signed off on it? Come on.” He waits a moment as Mike on the other line speaks. “Okay, great. I’ll check back with you next week when you have something. Thanks, buddy.” Dan hangs up the phone, then leans back in his chair slightly and breathes deep once, then again catching his breath.

* * *

CHAPTER NINE

The Year Is 2018

Samantha is speeding down a moonlit road in a blacked out top of the line, two-door Mercedes. The road is bordered by a tall stone wall. She drives next to the wall for what seems like forever until she comes up to an enormous, steel-gated entryway. She slows down just enough to whip the Mercedes into the small driveway in front of the steel gates and slams the brakes on stopping exactly next to an intercom mounted in the stone wall. The blacked out window of the car slides down and she extends her hand to push a button on the intercom. "Open the gates," Samantha says into the intercom.

The intercom beeps and the massive gates start to open.

Down the street from the gated entrance, hidden in the dark, sitting on the side of the road is Dan, in his car with binoculars, watching Samantha pull up through the gate. Dan Smiles under his binoculars, as he mumbles to himself "What the fuck is she doing here?"

Samantha continues up the long driveway for a minute, far behind the walls and steel gates. The driveway is lined with giant trees and thick bushes, before reaching the massive estate home of Gabriel. Samantha parks her car and flings the door open. Out comes Samantha in red high hills and a small black dress, looking hot and ready to hit the town for a night out. She walks up to two large, double doors to the front of the house, black with steel security bars bolted on them. As she approaches, the doors open with the sounds of a bank vault unlocking. Gabriel is standing inside and motions for her to come in.

Samantha enters the house, and the front door shuts behind her. Gabriel and Samantha walk down a hallway covered with beautifully framed pieces of art. They emerge from the hallway and into an oversized living room.

In the living room is a long, red couch with a coffee table in front of it and end tables on each side, in front of the table is a floor-to-ceiling window. The window faces out at the back of the compound and during the daylight, one would be able to see a large thick forest of trees that stretch for miles, but at night black darkness is all that is visible through the window.

"You made it here quick," Gabriel says. "I would ask if you even went home first, but looking at you, I know you did. Very nice."

"Well, thank you," Samantha says. "Why aren't you ready? The night is wasting."

"Give me a minute, and I'll be ready to go," Gabriel walks away, down another long hallway in the house.

Samantha walks over to the couch and leans against it looking out at the darkness. In a few seconds, Gabriel walks back in the room but is now wearing a sharp, black suit, no tie, and the top of his shirt unbuttoned. She turns to admire him. "You always clean up very well."

"You have seen me in a suit a million times," Gabriel replies with a smirk.

Samantha walks over to Gabriel and sensually rubs her hand up the front of his chest. "Yes, I have," Samantha says, "and it always makes me feel the same way."

As Gabriel and Samantha look at each other, a mischievous smile starts creeping across Samantha's face to match his. "You know, we shouldn't even be going out tonight," Gabriel says.

"No, we shouldn't be making new drugs," Samantha's smile fades.

"But we are, so this is going to be the last time we do this for a while, till this FDA stuff passes, and we can go back to the shadows again," Gabriel says, "hopefully for good this time."

"I know," Samantha says. "That's why tonight should be special; we should go all out!"

"No, we shouldn't be going out at all," he says. "Why do I let you talk me into this shit?"

"Because you love it too," Samantha says and leans in closer to him. "Come on let's get going, the night is wasting. Is the car here?"

They walk outside of the house to a long, black limousine waiting in the driveway. Samantha takes Gabriel's hand into hers as they make their way to the vehicle.

The limousine driver, who is standing by the back, opens the door for Samantha and Gabriel to climb in. The limousine slowly pulls away from the house and down the driveway, then turns onto the main street outside of Gabriel's compound.

In his car, still watching, Dan perks up as he sees the limousine pull out from the gates. He adjusts himself to a driving position with both hands on the steering wheel and his heart starts to beat faster. Without even thinking about it the fingers on his right-hand start to slowly roll on the steering wheel, index, middle, ring and pinky till he pushes on the gas pedal and grips the wheel tight as his car pulls off the side of the road to follow the limousine.

Inside the limousine, the driver speaks through the small window that divides the driver from the passengers, "Where to tonight, sir?"

"So, I'm sure you have this planned out," Gabriel says to Samantha. "Where too?"

"Houston, we are going to a new club called Prohibition," Samantha says.

"Very good, ma'am," the driver says and rolls the small window up leaving the two in privacy.

Thirty minutes of driving passes and the limousine pulls slowly past a long line of people waiting to get into the new hot spot in town, Prohibition night club. The limousine comes to a stop at the front entrance of the club, and the driver exits to open the door for Gabriel and Samantha. The line of people falls silent as they watch Gabriel and Samantha exit the limousine and walk toward the two bouncers standing at the front door of Prohibition. Both bouncers look like bodybuilders in nice suits. The first bouncer holds his hand out towards Gabriel and Samantha in the stop what you're doing position.

"Look at these two silly fucks," the first bouncer says to the other.

The bouncer walks a few feet away from the door of Prohibition towards Gabriel and Samantha, but not past the safety of the red velvet ropes separating him from them. "I don't care if you paid for a limo or not," he says, "the line starts back there." He points to the end of the long line of people waiting to get in the night club. Samantha reaches past the velvet ropes and seductively rubs the inside of the bouncer's forearm, then gently wraps her hand around his wrist. He looks annoyed, thinking Samantha, is just another party girl wanting in the club for free or to skip the line. Suddenly, a look of pain and confusion takes over the bouncer's face, as Samantha squeezes down on his wrist like a vice grip. He looks at Samantha realizing that it is her increasingly crushing his wrist.

Samantha pulls him to her with ease, almost making him fall over the red velvet ropes. She looks deep into his eyes. He is frozen, motionless, expressionless, and thoughtless, mesmerized now and forgetting about the pain in his forearm. "No, honey," She says with a smile on her face, "We have a reservation. Show us in now, please."

The bouncer is unable to do anything but what he is told to do by Samantha. She releases the bouncer's wrist.

"Yes, of course," he says. "Right this way," still expressionless.

He unhooks the velvet rope and walks Samantha and Gabriel to the front door, right past the other bouncer.

"What the fuck are you doing?" the second bouncer asks the first bouncer.

The still expressionless bouncer ignores the second bouncer and opens the door to Prohibition for Gabriel and Samantha. They enter the club and the door shuts behind them.

Dan seeing Gabriel and Samantha enter the club from across the street makes his move and walks up to the bouncers who are arguing with each other now.

"What the fuck are you talking about?" The first bouncer asks. "What guy in a black suit? I've been sitting right here?"

"Hey guys, can I have a word with you?" Dan asks which interrupts the two bouncers arguing.

"The line is back there, buddy, and if you're here looking for your daughter, that's on you," the second bouncer says with a smirk on his face and points to the end of the long line.

The first bouncer walks over to Dan.

"Tell your friend to fuck off, I'm not looking for my daughter!" Says a very irritated Dan.

"What do you need, man?" The bouncer asks.

"I am actually here doing a little work, I need to get inside," Dan pulls out his wallet and flips his FDA badge out for the bouncer to see.

"What does that say?" The bouncer asks as he looks at the badge. "You're not a city cop."

"Yeah, that's right buddy, I'm a Fed, it's an FDA badge," Dan explains, pointing at his badge.

"Well, I don't know what the FDA is, so unless that badge comes with a hundred spot, the line is back there, buddy," the bouncer says and points to the end of the line, which is even longer now.

Even more irritated now, Dan closes the badge part of his wallet and opens a pocket in the wallet that holds money. All that is in it is a single twenty-dollar bill that he slowly pulls out and then looks the bouncer in the eyes.

A smile grows on the bouncer's face. "A twenty?" the bouncer huffs. "Come on, guy. You can't even catch a buzz with that if I let you in. Hit the road, buddy." The bouncer turns and walks back to join the second bouncer leaving Dan standing alone. Dan looks over at the line of young people waiting to get in, but this time, he sees Martha Ellis near the front of the line. Dan puts his wallet away frustrated and beat and walks back across the street to his car.

Inside the club, two bottle service girls stand next to a VIP host, Brad who looks sharp, dressed in a red pinstriped suit with a black tie. "Good evening, and welcome to Prohibition," Brad says. "My name is Brad. I will be your VIP host for the evening."

"Perfect, Sweetie, we would love a table," Samantha says.

"Right this way," Brad says. "I have a nice table right next to the DJ, where everyone will see you."

Gabriel leans over to Brad as they walk and whispers into his ear. "I think we would like something a little more private."

"I think, I know what you mean," Brad says. "So, a table for the two of you this evening?"

"No, sweetie," Samantha says. "We will be having other people join us. Let's say a table for six tonight."

Brad smiles, thinking of the tip he is going to make on a bigger table, "Right this way. I have just the right spot for you two."

Brad leads them from the smaller entry room into the main area of the club. The dance floor is packed with people, lights going on and off like fireworks on the 4th of July, the music so loud it vibrates their bodies. Brad stops at the last VIP booth in the corner of the room. The lights don't reach this booth, it is dark and private.

"A VIP girl will be right back to take care of your orders," Brad says and walks away.

Gabriel sits on the low red couch and stretches out. Samantha straddles him with both hands on his shoulders. Gabriel slides his hands up Samantha's hips and onto her waist.

"This isn't turning out to be the relaxing evening I was hoping for," Gabriel says.

A VIP girl walks up to the table, she is thick and very voluptuous with all the right curves. She leans in over the table exposing her large cleavage to Gabriel. This girl is quick-witted and knows the bar game like the back of her hand.

"Hello, I'm Veronica," the VIP girl says as she runs her hands along her seductive curves. "I'll be your server tonight. What can I start you two with?"

Veronica sits down on the couch ready to take their order. Samantha is still straddled on top of Gabriel.

Veronica is Gabriel's type and Samantha knows it. She leans close to Gabriel's ear and whispers with a giggle "Did the night just start to get better for you?"

Gabriel smiles at Veronica. "Hello there, why don't you start us with whatever you like to drink."

"Thanks, I would love to have drinks with you two," Veronica says as she moves a little closer to Gabriel, "but the management here frowns on employees drinking at work."

Samantha reaches over and sensually rubs Veronica's arm. "Don't worry about that, Gabriel has a way of talking to people. I'm sure your manager will be fine honey."

"Yeah, go ahead and surprise us with your favorite bottle," Gabriel says.

"Okay, you guys asked for it," Veronica replies. "I'm a vodka girl; Grey Goose it is!"

Veronica starts to get up to leave, but Samantha grabs her wrist and gives her a seductive glare. "If you bump into any of your friends on the way, invite them over, we have plenty of room."

"What kind of party are you two looking for?" Veronica asks with a small chuckle as she puts her finger on the side of her nose and taps. Gabriel and Samantha look at each other and give a little smile.

"No, baby," Samantha says. "Not that kind of party for us, but we don't care if others partake in that."

"So, what are you looking for?" Veronica asks.

"Just pretty people that like to stay up all night and have a good time," Samantha answers. "Of course, all the drinks will be on us, cutie."

Veronica smiles brashly, "I know a lot of those kinds of people. Let me see what I can find tonight in the club for you."

As Veronica leaves to get their drinks, Samantha slides one hand down Gabriel's chest and onto his crotch, Gabriel looks at her smiling. "See, now I know the old Gabriel is still in there."

A few minutes later Veronica returns carrying a VIP setup with a bottle of vodka in it. A second, cute VIP girl is carrying mixers and ice for the drinks. Veronica and the second VIP girl start to set up the table. Samantha gets off Gabriel and sits next to him, watching the girls set up the drinks.

"I talked to a girl I kind of know that said she would like to have some drinks," Veronica says after finishing the table set up.

A tipsy, Martha Ellis, walks up to the table. "Is this where the vodka is?"

Veronica looks at Gabriel for approval, he nods, and Veronica starts making them all drinks.

Martha sits next to Samantha. Veronica finishes the first drink and hands it to Martha. "Martha, right?" Veronica asks.

"Yep, that's me," Martha says with a slight hiccup. "Martha Ellis."

"What a beautiful girl you are, Martha," Samantha says with a gentle tone. "This is my friend Gabriel."

Gabriel looks over at Martha and holds out his hand. Martha extends her hand and Gabriel kisses the top of her hand. Samantha rests her hand on Martha's thigh. Martha already half-drunk doesn't seem to mind Samantha's hand on her.

"Hello, Gabriel," Martha says.

Veronica hands Gabriel a drink and their hands touch in the exchange, "Wow, your hand is a little cold."

"It's a cold night," Gabriel replies.

"It's actually kind of warm in here," Veronica protests, then she and the other VIP girl leave the area.

Samantha and Gabriel both set their full drinks down on the table at the same time and Samantha says "So, let's all have some drinks and get to know each other."

The music gets louder as they start talking to each other. The group talks and chats about local news and small chitchat. Veronica continues to check on them through the out the night. After several hours Veronica walks back to the VIP table with the tab in her hand. Martha is sitting in between Gabriel and Samantha now enjoying her night. Veronica walks past the table and sits next to Gabriel.

"It looks like you had a pretty good evening," Veronica says. "I can just leave the tab on the table for you."

"Yes, we have had a very good evening, but the night is still young," Gabriel says and puts his arm around Veronica to pull her closer. "So, here's the thing, me and my friend Samantha, want to keep partying, and Martha here wants to keep partying also, but she doesn't really know us and would probably feel better about coming back to my place if you were coming, as well."

"So, here's the thing," Veronica smartly replies. "I don't really know her that well, and I don't know you two at all. So, what's in this for me? You going to make it worth my while?"

"Of course, I would be happy to," Gabriel says with a smile.

"A thousand to come over, and two more for anything else," Veronica says with a look at Gabriel that says the price isn't negotiable.

"I think we have a deal young lady," Gabriel says. "Here's the deposit." Gabriel reaches in his pocket and pulls out a wad of hundred-dollar bills. He peels off several of the hundreds from the wad and tucks them into Veronica's bra. Veronica stands up with a smile.

"It's going to take me a little bit to get out of here," Veronica says and looks over at all the VIP tables still full of people.

'I'm sure it will be quicker tonight," Gabriel says. "Your manager is Brad, right?"

"Yeah, that's right," she says and walks away.

Gabriel gets up and motions for Samantha to follow. Samantha pushes the bottom of Martha's drink up to her mouth, and then gets up and follows Gabriel a few feet away from Martha.

"Let's get out of here," Gabriel says. "Grab her and meet me outside."

"See you in a minute," Samantha says with a wink from her eye.

They smile at each other. Samantha seductively motions for Martha to come with her, and they quietly walk into the crowd holding hands. Meanwhile, Gabriel walks through the club looking for Brad, who he sees standing near the front entrance. Gabriel grabs Brad's arm and quickly pulls him close, looking into Brad's eyes. "You have too many people working tonight, and you don't need Veronica to stay any longer," Gabriel says with his penetrating stare. "Go tell her to leave for the night. You also never saw me or my friend tonight." Gabriel let's go of brad, who walks off looking confused.

Outside, Gabriel, Samantha and Martha meet with each other as the limousine pulls up. Gabriel opens the door, and Samantha and Martha get in. Veronica walks out of the club and over to the Limousine.

"Crazy, Brad said they didn't need me to help close tonight," Veronica says. "You didn't have anything to do with that did you?"

"Me, no I didn't have anything to do with that," Gabriel says with a smile and gestures for her to get inside of the limousine, she climbs in followed by Gabriel, and he closes the door as the limousine pulls away from the curb.

The limousine pulls up to the front of Gabriel's house and Gabriel, Samantha, Martha and Veronica all exit the vehicle and walk toward the front doors.

"Wow, this is an awesome house!" Martha says.

"Wait till you see the inside, I think you guys will really like it and later I'll show you both the forest behind the house," Gabriel says with a laugh.

"I should have told you five thousand," Veronica says as she is in awe of the mansion.

"Don't worry, you will definitely be getting what you have coming to you," Gabriel says with an evil smile.

The limousine pulls away and drives down the long driveway away from the house.

"Hey, how are we going to get home now?' Martha asks as she points at the limousine leaving the driveway.

Samantha wraps her arm around the now drunk Martha, to guide her into Gabriel's house, "You are home, honey," Samantha says. The four of them enter the house, and the double doors close and lock tight behind them. When they enter the living room, Gabriel closes the shades cutting off their view of the outside world.

"Let me get you, ladies, a drink and give you a tour," Samantha says. "Is red wine okay?"

Gabriel takes his jacket off and throws it on the back of the couch. Samantha returns from the kitchen and hands the girls each a big glass of red wine.

"Right this way, ladies," Samantha says and leads them all down a long hallway, filled with closed doors. She stops at a closed green door that has an over-sized deadbolt lock on it. "Just boring rooms and bathrooms and useless spaces down there," as she points down the long hallway. "But this room is special," Samantha says. "Would you two like to see it?"

"What's in it?" Martha asks as she takes a drink from her wine glass.

"Fun..." Samantha opens the large heavy door and turns to face the girls in the hallway, slowly backing into the dark room while motioning with her index finger for the girls to follow her into the room.

The girls follow Samantha into the room. Veronica is quick to flip on the light switch once they are in the room. Both the girls stop and stare at the room. Ropes and chains hanging from the walls and the ceilings. A red plush couch with hand restraints tied to one end of it. In the corner is a cage with a locking wire door just big enough for a human to fit in. They are standing in the middle of a fetish dungeon!

"Holy shit! What the fuck!" Martha's excitement is overwhelming. She walks around the room and starts to touch everything in the room. "I have heard of shit like this but never thought I would see it," Martha says.

"You want to play some?" Samantha says to Martha as she steps closer to her and rubs the back of her neck.

"Fuck yes, but no whips or pain, okay?" Martha says as she enjoys Samantha rubbing her neck "I want to play but nothing rough, okay?"

"Of course, honey," Samantha says. "Let's try this, sweetie. I know you will like it. Samantha starts to tie Martha to a large wooden cross, bolted against a wall.

Veronica finishes her drink in one long gulp, then throws her purse onto a red leather chair. Veronica rubs Gabriel's arm and then his shoulder as she turns to leave the room. "I should have started drinking when you guys did," Veronica says. "I have some catching up to do if I'm going to keep up with all of this. I'm going to get another glass of wine, and I'll be right back. This is looking like a long night."

With a nod of approval from Gabriel, Veronica leaves the room. Gabriel walks over and starts helping Samantha tie up Martha.

"Did you just let that girl leave?" Samantha asks.

"She is fine, the house is locked down, and her phone is in here in her purse," Gabriel says. "Where could she go?"

"What do you mean?" Martha asks.

Gabriel grabs Martha's head with both hands and starts kissing her before she can finish her sentence. Martha's eyes close with pleasure, enjoying the moment-until suddenly her eyes open wide in shock. A small line of blood runs down her chin. Gabriel stops kissing her and pushes her head back some to look at the line of blood that drips from her chin onto her cleavage, then pulls her head back to lick the blood from her lips.

"Ouch!" Martha shouts. "That fucking hurt, am I bleeding?"

Samantha, now overwhelmed with excitement, tears open Martha's shirt and bra. One of Martha's naked breasts hangs out.

"What the fuck!" Martha shouts. "I said nothing rough, and you just ripped a $50-dollar bra, and my shirt! Bitch, untie me!" Martha is quickly sobering up now to realize this isn't the fun and games she was expecting.

Martha struggles in her restraints, helpless. Gabriel and Samantha are both overcome with excitement. Samantha rubs Martha's naked breast. While Gabriel focuses in on Martha's neck, as she struggles Gabriel grabs a full hand of Martha's hair and slams her head against the wood cross she is tied to. Martha's eye rolls back in her head for a moment semi-unconscious before she comes back to life.

Samantha's fangs come out with a snap, and she bites deep into Martha's breast, a thin line of blood runs in between her cleavage.

Gabriel's fangs snap out, and he bites deep into the side of Martha's neck. Two lines of blood run down her neck and join the blood in her cleavage. The two of them are like sharks in a feeding frenzy.

Oblivious of what is happening in the room with the green door, Veronica turns on the lights in the kitchen and walks over to the half-empty bottle of wine sitting on a counter, she pours a full glass of wine and then puts her hand under the ice dispenser on the refrigerator door, waiting for a chunk of ice to cool her wine, but nothing comes out. She opens the freezer door; no light comes on and no food is in it. She opens the other fridge door and it's the same, no light, no food. Veronica shuts the doors and immediately moves over to a cabinet, stops and stares at the closed door, then slowly opens it, empty, then another cabinet, then another, all empty. Nothing at all, no food, no plates, no cups, just empty. She spins around surveying the countertop. Everything looks normal, but then she sees a wood block that would normally have knives in it, also empty.

First, a feeling of confusion, then a feeling of fear takes over her! Veronica knows something is wrong with this house and her hosts. She starts to walk toward the front door but stops and notices that what was the floor-to-ceiling window she looked out when they come into the house earlier is now covered with a steel roll down security shutter, and there are no other windows to be seen. She now knows she is locked in the house.

In the other room, Martha is still moaning and squirming to get free while Gabriel slowly slides his large hand over Martha's mouth to silence her moans and pleas to stop.

"You should probably go get our little friend in the kitchen," Samantha says. Before taking another deep bite into Martha's underarm that is securely tied to the cross.

Gabriel and Samantha laugh. Gabriel is gone from the room in a flash. In the front entryway of the house, Veronica is frantically trying to open the front door, then sensing she is no longer the only person in the room, stops and slowly turns around to see Gabriel looking at her from the other side of the room.

"Please don't," Veronica begs. "I swear I won't say anything."

"What about your friend?" Gabriel asks as he takes a step toward her. "Were you just going to leave her?"

"I don't even really know her," Veronica says as tears well in her eyes. "I swear, I won't tell anyone I was here, please."

"Aww, now that's not being a good friend," Gabriel laughs, and he takes another step toward her like a cat would if it had a mouse in a corner.

Gabriel closes the remainder of the distance between them at super speed and grabs her by the hair before she can even blink her eyes, to drag her back to the room with the green door. Veronica screams and struggles to escape, but Gabriel has done this to many times before to let her get away from him.

Gabriel enters the room, holding Veronica by her hair as she struggles to get free. Samantha stops biting Martha and looks up at them.

"Look who I found, trying to leave the party early," Gabriel says. With his arm extended lifts Veronica a few inches off the ground by her hair holding her suspended in the air. Then like throwing a pillow on a couch, Gabriel throws Veronica into the room and onto the floor. Gabriel walks further into the room and shuts the door behind him, locking it.

"Tonight, the two of you never had any drinks at the club!" Veronica shouts as she gathers herself. "Why is there no food or anything in the kitchen!"

Samantha let's go of Martha who is fading in and out of consciousness and walks over to Veronica looking down at her intensely.

"Because our food came home with us," Samantha says looking hard at the shaking and trembling Veronica who is still on the ground.

Veronica looks over at the bitten and bloody Martha tied to the cross and says "Vampires? are you fucking kidding me? For real!"

Samantha looks at Gabriel with a smile.

"Yes, we are definitely real and very hungry," Gabriel says.

"Are you ready to join your friend Martha in the fun?" Gabriel asks as his razor-sharp fangs snap out again.

* * *

Hours later, Gabriel and Samantha are standing outside in the darkness at the edge of a large wooded area with smaller trees that gradually turn into tall trees as you go further in. It's the beginning of the forest that could be seen from Gabriel's living room window. In front of them are two deep holes they've just finished digging. Next to each hole is what looks like a body wrapped in plastic and duct tape.

"We need to finish this up, it's getting close to dawn," Gabriel says as he looks at the lightening sky.

"You know, we don't have to stay here with Azreal and the others," Samantha says. "We can leave and just continue to have fun wherever we want to go, anywhere in the world."

"We need to stop for a while Samantha and let things die down," Gabriel says as he glances down at the bagged bodies laying on the ground next to them. "This was our last night like this for a while."

"It doesn't have to be!" Samantha pleads and tries to place her hand on him, but he shrugs her off.

"Just finish up we don't have very much time till dawn," Gabriel says.

Samantha laughs, "It's your fault, you played with these little mice too long this time my big cat."

The first rays of the sun start to peak over the foothills. Samantha and Gabriel look at each other. They start moving incredibly fast in a tornado of motion, throwing the body's in the holes and then filling them almost all the way full of dirt. Then quickly set a small tree on top of each hole before finishing filling them with dirt.

The sun almost cresting the foothills behind the forest now. Gabriel and Samantha run fast as lighting back to the garage connected to Gabriel's house just as the first rays of sunlight hit the driveway, almost chasing them into the garage. Gabriel walks over to a floor sink and washes his arms and then his shovel. Next to the sink is a bottle of bleach that he pours over the shovel.

Gabriel turns to see Samantha standing there looking at him. She doesn't have her shovel.

"Where is it? How could you have forgotten your shovel?" Gabriel asks aggressively.

"It's not a big deal," Samantha says. "I'll get it tomorrow night, no one is coming here."

* * *

CHAPTER TEN

The Year Is 2018

In the Old World Pharmaceuticals parking lot Dan's black, a four-door sedan pulls in and parks, followed by Frank's sedan. Dan exits his vehicle first and buttons up his jacket as a cold breeze blows past him. Frank gets out of his car next, and they both walk toward the front of the Old World Pharmaceuticals building.

"Why are we here, Dan?" Frank asks. "Does Angela know we're here?"

"Yeah, it's all good," Dan says over his shoulder to Frank. "I just have a few follow up questions. We will be in and out, don't worry so much fucking new guy."

Dan and Frank walk in. The receptionist is sitting at her desk, watching the same wall screen TV again. She hardly notices Dan walking up to her desk. Frank sits in the waiting area and starts watching TV.

"Déjà vu, huh?" Dan says.

The receptionist stops watching TV to look at Dan, "Huh?"

"Never mind," Dan says. "I need to see your bosses for a minute."

The receptionist flips through her appointment book in front of her, "I don't see any appointments for today. Do you have an appointment?"

"It's okay, are your bosses here?" Dan asks. "This will only take a minute."

"Have a seat and I will check," the receptionist turns to look out the window at the sun setting.

Dan turns and walks over to sit down next to Frank. They both look up at the TV.

On the television a single news anchor sitting at his desk reports, "It looks like we have another update on the latest in a series of missing persons reported. Let's go live, now, to Houston PD."

The TV show cuts to the briefing area inside the Houston Police Department. The public relations officer and Jacob Ellis walk to a podium.

"We have had some new developments in our missing person's case," the public relations officer says. "Unfortunately, we have had two new cases reported over the weekend."

"Can you give us any other new details?" a reporter asks.

"Yes, the names of the two new cases are Martha Ellis and Veronica Sanchez," the public relations officer says. "They were both reported last seen at Prohibition, a nightclub in downtown. We think these two girls may have come into contact with the subject or subjects we are seeking in the other cases."

Jacob Ellis, in wrinkled clothes, looks like he has been awake for a few days, leans in closer to the microphone to talk after the Public Relations officer, then holds up a picture of Martha Ellis.

"This is my sister Martha, if anyone has seen her please contact me, or the police department, please!" Jacob says while holding up his sister's picture for the camera to see.

The Public Relations Officer places his hand on Jacobs' shoulder and then leans back to the microphone.

"So, is this a serial killer case?" another reporter asks.

Jacob uncontrollably breaks into tears at the sound of the question.

"We are still hopeful all these girls will be found alive and well," the public relations officer says. "If anyone has any information, please call our hotline."

Dan looks from the screen back at Frank with a surprised look and says, "I know it is that mother-fucker!"

"What the fuck, that was Jacob and a picture of his sister, that answered the door for us," Frank says stupefied.

"Yeah, I know, I saw her Friday night at that club," Dan says.

"What do you mean, you saw her?" Frank asks, then turns to look Dan in the eyes. "Why would you be at that club, Dan?"

Dan says, "I was doing a little surveillance, and I followed Gabriel and a girl who works here to that club."

"What the fuck, Dan, Angela doesn't know we are here, huh?" Frank demands. "She damn sure doesn't know you are doing your own surveillance, does she?"

"Keep your voice down and just relax, FNG. We are going to get these bastards, I know it," Dan says.

"Fuck Dan, you're going to get you and me fired!" Frank says.

The receptionist hangs up the phone, then looks over at Dan and Frank, "You don't have an appointment, but they will see you anyway."

* * *

Dan and Frank enter the conference room and take seats at the table. Azreal, Gabriel, and Haley are already sitting on the other side of the table.

"Good evening, agents," Azreal says while tapping the fingertips of both hands together in front of him with his elbows on the table. "What can we do for you?"

"I just have a few follow up questions," Dan says.

"Next time you have questions, you should make an appointment," Gabriel snaps at Dan.

"Yeah, I'll make sure and do that next time," Dan says directly at Gabriel. "So, how was your weekend, Gabriel?"

Dan places his hand on the table, and rolls his fingers slowly, then leans forward. The others glance at his fingers as he wraps them against the table over and over.

"I had a great weekend, but that's not what your here for," Gabriel says.

"Really?" Dan replies and raises an eyebrow at Gabriel. "So, what did you do this weekend Gabriel?"

Gabriel leans back in his chair thinking about the question and looking at Dan.

"If you don't have anything business related to talk about, we can end this meeting right now, agent," Azreal says as he looks over at Gabriel.

"So, yeah okay, let's move on," Dan says. "Did you guys get that list of compounds for XP1 that we asked for at the last meeting?"

"You know that list was submitted with our application for XP1," Azreal calmly replies.

"No, I mean the one with all the compounds on it!" Dan shouts back at Azreal. "Not that partial one you submitted! Come on guys lets quit fucking around here okay."

"Both of you get up and get out!" Haley shouts at them as she abruptly stands up from her seat shoving it back a few feet and walks with a purpose around the table and straight at Dan and Frank.

Frank frantically gets up as fast as he can to get away from Haley oncoming approach.

"Come on, Dan, this is over, get up," Frank says and grabs Dan out of his chair and onto his feet, then guides him toward the door with both hands-on Dan's shoulders.

"Don't think this is over for any of you!" Dan shouts as he's led away from the table by Frank "Not by a long shoot!"

Frank continues to push Dan toward the door. He opens it as quick as he can to get Dan out of the room. Haley follows them close behind all the way to the door and slams it behind them, almost hitting Frank.

Azreal springs to his feet in the blink of an eye then turns and lunges at Gabriel grabbing him by the arm and the neck, pinning him in his chair with such force it would have crushed a regular human's bones. The chair rocks from side to side as Azreal pushes it across the room with Gabriel trapped in it struggling to free himself, until the chair comes to an abrupt stop, slamming against a wall.

"What did you do over the weekend, Gabriel?" Azreal shouts as he leans his face closer to Gabriel's face, they are almost nose to nose now. "Tell me, Gabriel!"

"Nothing," Gabriel shrieks back. "I swear nothing!"

"You're lying!" Azreal says and tightens his grip. "I can see it in your eyes! You're back to your old ways, aren't you? I know it."

Azreal slowly releases his hold of Gabriel and backs up looking down at Gabriel still in the chair. Then, he turns back toward the conference table and walks over to it, slamming both of his hands on the table.

* * *

CHAPTER ELEVEN

The Year Is 1986

Azreal, Samuel, Gabriel, and Senator Thatch are on a walkway that leads to a large house. The door to the house opens as they are walking up. Senator O'Hara an averagely looking man in his fifties is standing inside the open door. "I don't know why you wanted to meet so late, so this better be good."

"Believe me," Senator Thatch says, "this will be a meeting you will never forget. Is Myrick here?"

"Yes, he is here and just as annoyed as I am," Senator O'Hara barks back. "He is in the living room, waiting. And what does my son have to do with this?"

"You going to invite us in?" Senator Thatch asks while still standing outside the door with the others.

"Who are these guys with you?" Senator O'Hara asks.

"This is Azreal, Samuel, and Gabriel, they need you to invite them into your home," Senator Thatch says and then walks past Senator O'Hara to enter the house.

"Come on in, I guess," Senator O'Hara says to the others.

A few minutes later inside the house in Senator O'Hara's living room, there are several over-sized chairs surrounding a long coffee table. Sitting in the chairs are Senator Thatch, Senator O'Hara, and Senator Myrick, a short stocky man in his forties. Azreal, Samuel and Gabriel sit on a couch facing the Senators.

"So, why the cloak-and-dagger stuff at this hour of the night?" Senator Myrick asks as he takes a drink from the teacup he is holding. He looks as if sleep is already dragging at his eyelids.

"They need our help, and we definitely need theirs, but it's better if I just let you two hear and see it from them," Senator Thatch says to the group.

"Senator O'Hara, I understand you have a sick son?" Azreal asks. "Steven, right? We would like to help him."

"Thanks, I appreciate that, but we already have the best doctors in the county that specialize in childhood cancers taking care of him," Senator O'Hara says, then takes a slight gulp.

"We aren't doctors, and we don't specialize in cancer," Azreal says, "but what if I told you we had something that could completely cure your son and allow him to have a full and healthy life?"

* * *

In Steven O'Hara's bedroom, the late teen sits in his bed half-awake looking weak and pale. Standing at the head of his bed next to him is Senator O'Hara, and next to him is Samuel. Azreal, Gabriel, Senator Myrick, and Senator Thatch is standing some distance away from the bed.

"Hello Steven, my name is Samuel," Samuel says.

"Hello, Samuel," Steven takes his time to speak.

Samuel sits down on the bed next to Steven and says in a calm voice "Steven, I know you're sick, and I have something that I think will make you feel much better, would you like that? To feel better?"

"I'm going to be a scientist when I grow up, and I will find out what is causing me to be sick," Steven says as he tries to sit himself up.

"A scientist, huh?" Samuel says with a smile on his face. "Well, maybe when you're older we will work together. I think I would like that."

Steven smiles back at Samuel and Samuel rubs Steven's head. Then looks back at Senator O'Hara, who smiles as well. Samuel reaches into his vest pocket and pulls out a small, glass vile of blood that he hands to Steven.

"I need you to drink this and I promise tomorrow will be a whole new day for you, feeling much better," Samuel says.

Steven looks over at his father, Senator O'Hara who nods in approval. Steven gently takes the veil from Samuel and drinks the blood from it. Within a few seconds, the young man responds to the liquid as color begins to return to his face and he appears to hold his neck with a little more strength. The healing continues at a quick rate till Steven is unrecognizable from the sick child that he was moments ago.

The group of men leave Stevens room and make their way to the entrance of the house just inside the front door. Senator Myrick and Senator Thatch stop and turn to face Azreal, Samuel, and Gabriel. Their faces are awestruck.

"That was simply remarkable I wouldn't have believed it if I hadn't seen it with my own eyes," Senator Myrick exclaims.

"Good, so, you understand the need for our work to continue and to stay private," Azreal says.

"Yes, of course," Senator Myrick says. "I completely understand that now. If what you gentleman really are got out to the public, you probably wouldn't be safe anywhere."

"We take our privacy very seriously," Samuel says. "We have a lot at stake, and we need to keep things as confidential as possible."

"I understand what you want from me, and now, I understand why both of my colleagues are eager to help you, gentlemen," Senator Myrick looks at Senator Thatch. "But I'm not sick, and I don't know anyone that is sick, so what's in this for me? You three are about to become three of the richest people on the planet."

"Goddammit, Myrick!" Senator Thatch yells. "Are you seriously just thinking about yourself right now? Faster than light, Azreal reaches out and puts his hand on Senator Myrick's shoulder. He gently squeezes it more and more until Senator Myrick shows signs of pain.

Azreal says in a stern voice "What you say is true, but the reason we are doing this has nothing to do with money or worldly positions. The real reason is we all feel some level of guilt for the horrible things we have done to humans just like yourself for hundreds of years now."

"Let go of me!" Senator Myrick says as he tries to brush Azreal's hand off his shoulder, but Azreal's tight grip just forces him to lean over further in pain as he continues to squeeze the Senator's shoulder harder.

Azreal continues, "You are still human, though, and someday in the future, you will get sick, or someone you know and love will get sick and when that day comes, we will still be here to help you, I'm sure even you can understand the benefit in being our friend."

Azreal releases his grip on Senator Myrick's shoulder, allowing him to stand straight up again and speak unhindered. The Senator now angry and hurt rubs his shoulder and says "Yes, I completely understand the benefit of being your friend when that day comes, and rest assured I'm going to hold you to that!"

"I'm sure you will," Azreal replies.

"In the meantime, since you don't care about worldly positions, I think twenty-five per cent to us sounds fair," Senator Myrick demands.

Samuel opens the front door of the house. At the same time, Azreal nods to Senator Myrick in agreement and exits the house with Samuel. Gabriel turns back to face the Senators and quickly grabs Senator Myrick's other shoulder even harder than Azreal's grip almost breaking the Senator's shoulder then with a hard jerk brings the Senator close to Gabriel's mouth, so he can whisper in his ear. "Also, if you decide to tell anyone about us, I will kill you and everyone you love," then flashes his fangs with a smile for the other Senators to see.

"Come along, Gabriel, it's time to go," Azreal calls out to Gabriel from outside the house. Gabriel releases Senator Myrick and is out the front door of the house in a flash and walking with Azreal and Samuel down the street and away from the house into the darkness of night.

* * *

CHAPTER TWELVE

The Year Is 2018

Azreal is sitting at his desk inside Old World, looking through some papers and occasionally glances up to look out the window in his office at the full moon in the night sky. Steven walks in and sits in a chair.

"Good evening, sir, I worked through the weekend," Steven says, "and I was able to get a small batch of XP1 ready for you."

Steven pulls out a pill bottle and sets it on Azreal's desk. Azreal picks it up and studies it closely, spinning it in his hands. "Good work, Steven," Azreal says. "I know we could depend on you."

"If there is nothing else, sir," Steven says. "I'm going to take the night off and go home."

"No, this will do it, thank you, Steven," Azreal says.

Steven gets up to leaves Azreal's office but stops at the door and turns back around. "Oh, and Jacob called me on my cell phone, I guess he couldn't get through on my office line. Saying he won't be back to work, I think his sister got kidnapped or something. So, I guess that problem fixed itself."

"Kidnapped?" Azreal says and looks up from the pill bottle at Steven.

"He was upset when we talked so I'm not sure, she may be part of the missing person cases. Good night sir." Steven says, then turns and leaves the office, leaving Azreal in silence and his thoughts.

* * *

Dan is in his office, looking at his computer screen and slowly rolling his fingers on his desk when the phone rings. It's Mike Brown from the FBI.

"Hey, about that job you wanted to be done at Old World," Mike says through the phone speaker.

"Give me some good news, buddy," Dan says as he rolls his fingers faster on the desk and kicks his feet up to recline in his chair.

"I wish I had some," Mike says with a sigh. "I gave it to one of my guys, and I guess he fucked it up, so we didn't get anything for you this weekend."

"Nothing at all?" Dan asks. "Come on!"

"If it makes you feel any better, the guy fucked it up so bad that he was fixing their phone lines all weekend, so they couldn't get any calls at all, all weekend," Mike says trying to cheer up Dan.

"No, that doesn't make me feel better," Dan says. "Fuck. Let me know when you actually have something."

Dan slams the phone down, then looks over at the picture of him and his daughter that sits on the corner of his desk.

* * *

CHAPTER THIRTEEN

The Years Is 2018

Haley is in her office looking out the window and watching the rats which scurry in the cracks of the pavement and under the shroud of darkness. Azreal walks in and sits in a chair in front of her desk.

"Steven, got the job done," Azreal says. "We can call the Senator back and deliver his package to him now."

"That's good news," Haley says while watching a fat one squeeze between the edge of the parking lot and a rock. "I'll give him a call and set up the delivery."

"Let me know the details when you have them," Azreal sets the pill bottle on Haley's desk and leaves the office.

Haley sits down at her desk and picks up the pill bottle to look at it, then sets it back down and picks up her phone. She punches in some numbers and the phone rings on the other end until a male answer it." Hello"

"Hello, may I speak with Senator Myrick," Haley says into the phone. "This is Haley, he is expecting my call."

The phone is silent for a few seconds, then-Senator Myrick's voice blares through the speaker. "I knew the first time I saw you bastards that none of you could be trusted!"

"Senator, I have your package, and the new drug is on schedule for production," Haley says still eyeing the pill bottle in front of her and ignoring the harshness of Senator Myrick. "All I need from you now is where to deliver it."

"I tried calling you guys all weekend and no answer, nothing," Senator Myrick says angrily.

"Senator, we have an answering service that works all weekend, so it is unlikely we missed your call," Haley explains. "You should also know that this will be the last drug we produce. So, our business arrangement will be concluded after this. You and your colleagues will all receive your final payments from us."

"I don't care about our deal anymore, and you can go ahead and keep whatever you made for me now," Senator Myrick says.

"What do you mean, Senator?" Haley asks as her face contorts to a frown. "You no longer want the medicine you asked us for?"

"That isn't what I said," Senator Myrick barks back at her. "I no longer need the meds. My wife passed away Saturday night when I couldn't reach you on the phone! You remember our deal, right?"

"Senator, why didn't you contact us, and we could have given you blood to help your wife instead of the new drug and your profits from it.

"Aren't you listening?" Senator Myrick asks. "I did try and contact you as soon as I realized she didn't have the time we thought she would! But she is gone now, and I'm old, so your threats won't work any longer. You should just run now. Just run as fast as you can."

Senator Myrick slams the phone down hanging up on Haley. She sits in the silence of the room, still holding the phone and looking at the bottle of pills.

* * *

Dan is sitting in his desk, just staring at the old picture of him and his daughter, while leaning back in his chair. The phone rings and rings. Dan wipes his watery eyes, sits up straight in his chair, and puts the picture down to answer the phone.

“Yeah?” Dan whispers into the phone still trying to clear his throat.

“Are you the Agent in charge of the Old World case, Dan?” the voice of Senator Myrick comes through the phone.

“Yeah, I’m in charge of the Old World case,” Dan says and perks up. “Who is this?”

“I want you to listen very closely,” Senator Myrick says. “I’m going to help you with your investigation.”

“Oh, yeah, what kind of help?” Dan asks. “And who is this?”

“Just be quiet and listen. In the 1980s and ’90s, I was a U.S. Senator,” Myrick says. “The owners of Old World approached me and several other Senators with a deal to help them with their drugs.”

“A deal?” Dan asks as he fumbles to pull out a piece of paper and a pen. He scribbles as he listens.

“The owners of Old World are not what they appear to be,” Myrick says.

“You don’t say,” Dan says with a slight chuckle. “I had that hunch before I even met them. Go on with your story.”

“Vampires,” Myrick says.

Dan drops the pen then leans back in his chair and laughs, "So, who at Old World is having you call me? Gabriel? I hope you're getting a laugh out of this because I really am."

"Their newest drug submission has some ingredients in it that you can't identify, correct?" Myrick asks.

Dan straightens up again and says into the phone, "Yeah, that's right. How did you know that?"

"I have sent you a package that will help you end Old World and also protect yourself," Myrick says. "Good luck, Dan." The phone goes dead.

Dan hangs the phone up, then quickly picks it back up and dials a number. "Hey, Buddy, this is Dan with the FDA," Dan says as Jacob's voice answers on the other line. "I'm sorry to hear about your sister, but I think I might have a break in the Old World case."

"I don't care about Old World right now," Jacob says.

"Well, I think Old World might have something to do with your sister's disappearance," Dan says. "I'd like to meet you to talk about it."

Dan hangs up the phone then leaves his office. Down the hall, he stops and opens Frank's office door, who is sitting at his desk.

"You're not going to believe what some old guy just told me about Old World," Dan says as he walks in, he sees Angela sitting in front of Frank's desk and it stops him in his tracks.

"Angela, sorry," Dan says. "I didn't know you were here. I can come back later."

"Have a seat, Dan," Angela says. "We were just talking about you. So, what did you hear about Old World now?"

Dan sits in a chair next to Angela, "It's nothing really," he says.

"No, Dan, I would like to know what you're talking about?" Angela asks as she turns her chair to look at Dan more directly. "I told you that you were off the Old World case."

"You're going to get a kick out of this," Dan says trying to lighten the mood. "The guy who called me just now thinks the owners are vampires." Dan giggles. Angela just stares at him with a straight face while Frank looks at him with concerned eyes.

"I have been struggling with this decision because of your years with the Government," Angela says, "but your making this much easier on me now."

"What are you talking about, Angela?" Dan asks.

"The investigation that you have been running on Old World is completely outside of your scope, Dan!" Angela says as she lifts her hand with her index finger pointed straight at Dan. "Agent Brown from the FBI called me this morning to verify a wiretap that you ordered, without a warrant! And now, Frank tells me that you went back to Old World again!"

"Come on, Angela," Dan says. "You know I'm close to figuring out what these guys are up to."

"Enough, Dan!" Angela shouts. "You're on administrative leave right now pending a review of your actions in this case. I want you back in my office next Monday morning for a meeting on this after I figure out all the shit you have been starting!"

"Angela..." Dan pleads.

"Put your badge and your gun on the desk, Dan," Angela demands.

Dan pulls his gun out and slams it on the desk. Then takes his badge out and looks at it with sad eyes before setting it next to his gun.

"You're making a mistake, Angela," Dan yells. "You'll see." As he storms out of Franck's office.

* * *

Azreal is sitting at his desk. Haley walks in and sits in a chair on the other side of the desk. Haley takes out the bottle of XP1 pills and sets them on Azreal's desk for him to see.

"We have a problem with the Senator," Haley says.

"Myrick?" Azreal asks.

"He said he tried to call us here all weekend, but the phones were down," Haley says.

"That can't be, but Steven mentioned that also," Azreal says.

"That's what I thought too, so I checked on it, and he was right, the phones were down all weekend," Haley says.

"Our phones have never been down," Azreal says.

"They were this last weekend, and then just started working again on Monday," Haley says. "Our security is checking on what happened." Haley gets up and walks to the window to look out at the moon, but it hides behind a cloudy night sky.

"The real problem now is that we missed Myrick's calls over the weekend and didn't get the pills to his wife in time," Haley says. "His wife died over the weekend."

"Why didn't he tell us she was that close?" Azreal asks.

"Maybe greed knowing this is our last drug?" Haley says. "Maybe pride finally needing something from us? Who knows."

"So, what is his position with us now?" Azreal asks.

"He will most likely try and go public about us," Haley says. "After all these years, there is no telling what he has on us. It could be believable to the public, depending on what he has."

Azreal leans back in his chair and puts his hands together matching up the fingertips on both hands and sinking into thought. "Do you think he will listen to reason?" Azreal says.

"He is old now, and feels slighted by us," Haley says. "I think we have past damage control with him. As much as I hate this, we need to let Gabriel handle it now."

"Gabriel?" Azreal asks as his finger tap together. "Let me think about it."

"Whatever we do, it needs to be sooner, rather than later," Haley says and walks out of his office.

* * *

A tan car pulls up in front of Dan's house and a man wearing dark glasses and a suit gets out of the car holding a box. He walks up to Dan's front door and knocks. A minute later Dan opens the door.

"Dan Miller?" the man in the suit asks.

"Yeah, I'm Dan," Dan says.

The man in the suit gives Dan the box, "I have a gift for you from my employer, the Senator."

Dan stands at his doorway, looking at the box. The man in the suit turns and walks back to his car and leaves as quick as he came.

Dan watches as the car drives off, then looks down at the box he is holding. Dan shuts the door and walks to his kitchen table carrying the box with him. With curiosity killing him Dan grabs his pocket knife and opens the box on his kitchen table. Slowly he pulls out a full box of 9mm bullets and opens it. He takes one of the bullets out of the box and looks at it. "Silver tips?" Dan asks himself as he examines the other bullets in the box, one after another, all of them have silver tips.

Dan puts the box of bullets down on his table. He reaches back into the box again and pulls out a thick black folder filled with papers. He sets it next to the box of bullets. Next out of the box is a Glock

9mm gun to match the bullets from the box, which Dan also sets on the table.

Dan's wife, Krista Miller walks into the kitchen and places her hands on his shoulders rubbing them softly. A tall, older lady who was once probably very attractive but with years of sadness from the loss of her only daughter and the lack of sunshine from rarely leaving the house, she's not the woman she once was. "Who was at the door?" Krista asks in a shy and meek voice.

Krista stops rubbing Dan's shoulders, and he sits down, Krista takes a seat next to him at the table looking at the contents of the box scattered out on the table.

"It was some guy who works for a Senator," Dan says. "He gave me this box."

Dan has the folder open and is reading the papers inside it.

"What is it?" Krista asks still confused with the box.

Dan continues to read the papers, while Krista sits in silence next to him.

"I fucking knew it!" Dan says.

"What?" Krista asks. "What is it, Dan?"

“Fucking Old World!” Dan shouts with excitement. “But this is way more then I was expecting!”

Krista gets visibly upset and looks at Dan, “I don’t want to talk about that company anymore.”

“No, baby, this is good,” Dan says in a soft voice as he puts the folder down to reach out and comfort his wife by rubbing her shoulder. “We are finally going to get those bastards. Look at this stuff.” He starts showing her the stuff from the box while they talk.

* * *

CHAPTER FOURTEEN

The Year Is 1988

Azreal, Haley, and Gabriel stand next to a table in the lab at Old World. They are watching Samuel drain his blood from a self-inflicted bite on his forearm into a glass apothecary jar. Samuel looks over at Azreal with dizzy eyes, then let's go of his forearm spilling blood from it onto the table. Samuel grabs at the table unsuccessfully trying to catch himself from falling. Azreal, looks back at Samuel not understanding what he is seeing but knowing that something is definitely wrong. Haley also looks over with disbelief in her face as she moved as fast as a bullet through the air to catch Samuel before he loses consciousness, unable to hold himself up, he falls into Haley's arms.

"Let's get him on the couch in my office," Azreal says still shocked at what he is seeing.

With super speed, Azreal and Haley take Samuel to Azreal's office.

Azreal and Haley lay Samuel down on the couch. Slowly, Samuel wakes up. He tries to sit up but is too weak. Haley puts her hands-on Samuel's shoulders gently pushing him back to a comfortable spot on the couch "just rest a minute."

"The last time you drained your blood for these drugs, you looked weak to me," Gabriel says. As he studies Samuel's appearance.

"Yes, I have felt weaker every time, but after I feed, I feel fine and recover like always," Samuel replies in a weak voice.

Gabriel moves zips across the room and grabs Samuel's arm, then lefts it up to look at the bite marks on it.

"Not this time," Gabriel says.

Azreal and Haley look at the wound. It is still red and slowly closing. Under his arm is a blood stain on the couch.

"That should have been completely healed by now," Haley says as she looks closer at the bite.

"I knew this was crazy, helping humans!" Gabriel snaps.

"I hadn't noticed it till now, but your different," Azreal says. "You look as if you have aged."

Azreal, Haley, and Gabriel all look at Samuel closely, studying every detail in his face.

"What if we aren't immortal?" Haley asks as she rubs a small new wrinkle line next to Samuel's eye.

"What are you talking about?" Gabriel says. "Of course, we are."

"What if it has just appeared that way to us?" Haley says. "None of us have lived long enough to know what our lifespans really are."

"We might just be ageing slower, than humans," Samuel says. "Much slower."

"Or maybe losing this much blood has started your ageing again?" Gabriel says pointing at the wound.

"So, if I stop giving blood, then what?" Samuel asks as he looks at the others for answers.

"The damage may already be done," Gabriel says.

"If that is true, I welcome it," Samuel says. "At least, this way, I won't have to make the choice of carrying on or ending it again when Emma goes."

"From the looks of you now, you may get your wish," Gabriel says.

"This is a good thing!" Samuel Smiles. "And now we know that it can only be me who gives blood. It's too dangerous for any of you until we know how this will turn out."

* * *

The year is 2018

Samantha is hard to see as she speeds along in her Mercedes in the black night, she whips into the small driveway and stops the car in front of the massive steel gates that lead to Gabriel's estate. The intercom beeps after she pushes a button and the gates open. As the gates shut behind the black Mercedes, Dan and Jacob slip through the gate just before they close, on foot from the corner of the wall that they had been hiding behind. The two disappear into the tall trees and brush that line the driveway, undetected by anyone.

Samantha's tears up the driveway and stops in front of Gabriel's house. The car turns off, and she slams the door open to stand up outside of the car. Samantha slams the car door back shut and looks at herself in the reflection of the window, fixing her hair. She suddenly stops fixing her hair as she sees Dan and Jacob's reflection creep up in the window as they emerge from the bushes next to the driveway. Dan is breathing hard trying to catch his breath. Samantha turns around to face them and leans back against her car and puts both hands on her hips. At the sight of Dan and Jacob, she lets out a loud laugh. "Dan, you're a silly little boy, and you brought Jacob with you, even better. Why would mice come to a cat's house?"

Dan doubles over and puts his hands on his knees still trying to catch his breath. He lifts one hand to Samantha, palms out, in the stop motion.

"That's-that's-enough. Stop right there," Dan says still breathing hard.

"I'm not going anywhere, but what if I did?" Samantha says.

"What did you do with my sister?" Jacob yells.

"Who is your sister? Little mouse." Samantha asks.

"Dan told me you and Gabriel were at the night club with her last week!" Jacob says. "Martha!"

Samantha, giggles and takes a step toward Dan and Jacob.

"I think I know who you're talking about now, tasty little thing!" Samantha says and licks her lips. "Little fat boy, this might be the most fun I've had in a long, time. You two are going to be exciting!"

"What are you going to do?" Dan asks. "Kill us both as you did to those other girls, and who knows who else?"

Samantha takes another step toward Dan and Jacob. “Well, aren’t you the smart guy?” Samantha says still smiling big. “What is it that you think I have done, Dan?”

Dan straightens up. He is holding the gun from the Senator’s box at his hip, aimed in on Samantha.

“I know exactly what you and your co-workers have done,” Dan says. “You killed those girls and probably others!”

“Poor Dan,” Samantha says, “if you only know how many people we have killed, you would already have shot me. Too bad that isn’t going to stop me from draining every drop of blood from both of you fools.”

Gabriel opens the front door and sees Samantha, Dan, and Jacob in the driveway. He moves extremely fast and stops, standing a few feet away from Samantha and looking intently at Dan.

“I’ve been waiting for you to join us,” Dan says to Gabriel.

“Dan, you have no idea what’s about to happen to you and your friend!” Gabriel says.

Samantha looks over at Gabriel and they both laugh. Samantha takes another step toward Dan and Jacob. Jacob lunges at Samantha. Lighting fast Samantha grabs Jacob by his throat. Her fangs snap out, and she bites Jacob's neck tearing deep into the side of it and ripping a chunk of meat out before looking back at Dan!

Dan looks at Gabriel, then pulls the trigger, and with a flash from the muzzle, and a bang sends a silver slug hurtling at Samantha. The slug hits home under her ribcage. Forcing her to release Jacob and sending her stumbling back a few feet.

Samantha stops and looks down at the blood flowing from her stomach. Jacob stumbles away from her and puts his hand on his neck trying to stop his blood from spraying out. It's no use the bite is too deep. Jacob falls down shaking on the ground as he bleeds out looking at Samantha.

Faster than Dan can react, Gabriel is on top of him, seizing his gun hand and ripping the gun from it, then tossing it into the bushes next to the driveway. With speed and force, Gabriel spins Dan around and slams him to his knees. In Gabriel's face, anger and rage have now taken over.

One of Gabriel's powerful hands wrap around and squeeze Dan's throat. The other holds Dan's shoulder, forcing him to stay on his knees. Dan reaches up with both hands to try and free himself of Gabriel's grip on his throat, but he knows he is powerless to escape. Dan stops struggling and begins slowly rolling the fingers of his left hand on Gabriel's forearm, index, middle, ring, and pinky while he looks at Samantha still bleeding in front of him and Gabriel. Samantha falls to her knees, looking back at Gabriel and Dan. Then, with a gasp, Samantha catches fire and bursts into flames. She turns red, then blue, then purple. Dan smiles as Gabriel slowly squeezes the air from his throat. While both of their faces glow in dim and then bright light from the flames of Samantha. Dan goes limp, as Gabriel drops his lifeless body on the driveway. Next to Dan is Jacob, lifeless, still slowly bleeding out.

Gabriel steps over Dan and walks toward the ashes on the driveway that was Samantha. He falls to his knees in grief and then anger, rage in his eyes as he looks up at the night sky.

* * *

Angela and Frank knock on the front door of Dan's house. Krista answers the door. Her face is red, and her eyes are puffy and swollen, she has clearly been crying for some time now.

"Hello, Krista," Angela says.

"Yes?" Krista says after she calms her crying.

"I'm Angela, and this is Frank," Angela says. "Is Dan home at the moment?"

"No, he left to do some work and hasn't come home," Krista says.

"Do you mind if we come in to talk?" Angela asks. "Is this an okay time to talk?"

Krista opens the door wider for them to come in. Angela, Frank and Krista sit down around a coffee table in the living room. "It's not like Dan to not come home," Krista says as she chokes back tears and looks at a clock on the wall. "He has not come back home or called me in thirty years."

"Krista, Dan had a meeting with me today that he missed," Angela says. "Do you have any idea what he was working on when he left, or where he went?"

"Yes, he got a box from some guy," Krista explains. "I think he worked for a Senator?"

Krista gets up and walks into the kitchen. She comes back with the box and sets it on the coffee table.

"He got this a few days ago," Krista says.

Angela reaches in the box and pulls out the box of bullets. She hands it to Frank, then takes the stack of papers and sets them down to start reading through them. One by one, Angela skims through the papers. Frank opens the box of bullets and pulls one out to show

Angela, some of the bullets are missing. "Angela, I think this has a silver tip," Frank says.

Angela doesn't even hear Frank. She is focused on what's in the papers.

"What the fuck?" Angela mumbles to herself. "You have to be kidding me."

"What is it, Angela?" Frank asks and sets the box of bullets on the coffee table.

"I think this says the owners of Old World are vampires," Angela says. "Just like Dan was trying to tell us."

"I guess that would explain the silver bullets," Frank replies.

Angela stops reading and looks at Frank.

"Did you just say silver bullets?" Angela asks, and Frank lifts the same bullet up again for Angela to see.

"There was also a gun in the box," Krista says.

"Did Dan say where he was going, when he left?" Angela asks.

"I think he said, Gabriel? Maybe?" Krista says.

"We need to get this stuff back to the office," Angela says and starts to gather it all together.

* * *

Haley is sitting at her desk when Azreal opens her door and leans in.

"I've been looking for Gabriel and Samantha," Azreal says. "Have you seen them?"

"No, I haven't seen them in a few days," Haley shrugs. "I assumed you sent him to see the Senator?"

"No, that's actually what I wanted to talk to him about," Azreal says. "I think there might be another way. I'll find him, and we can all talk."

* * *

Samuel and Emma are lying in their bed. It's the wee hours of the morning right before daybreak. Emma is weak and in pain. She struggles to sit up. Samuel is now looking very old. He gently props her up and tucks pillows under her back. They both snuggle together and look into each other's eyes.

"I have lived for longer then I should have, thanks to you, my love," Emma says.

Samuel gently wipes her silver hair out of her eyes and tucks it behind her ear.

Emma explains "I want to carry on in this world for you, my love, but every day, I feel weaker, and the pain is greater."

Samuel slowly raises his forearm to his mouth. Emma rests her hand on top of his forearm, stopping Samuel from biting himself to feed her.

"No, my love, I think it's time," Emma snuggles into Samuel's chest and wraps her arms around him. Samuel holds Emma as tight as he can without hurting her.

"We have had a great life," Samuel says as he gazes down at her. "I have no regrets."

Samuel leans Emma back and places another pillow behind her. He gets up and walks across the room to the large, steel shutter that covers the floor-to-ceiling window in their room. With the push of a button, the shutter rolls up. A blackout curtain covers the window. Samuel looks back at Emma, who smiles at him.

"Go ahead, my love, I'm ready," Emma says.

Samuel slowly and deliberately opens one side of the curtains and tucks it on a hook to keep it open. He stops to look out at the darkness before opening the other side of the curtains and tucking them back on another hook. Samuel walks back to the bed and gets in. They both fall into each other's arms again and Emma rests her head on Samuel's chest with her eyes closed and at peace.

The sun approaches over a series of small foothills. Slowly, beams of light start to creep over the foothills and make their way to the house. The sun finally breaks over the top of the last hill and straight into the window of their bedroom. From outside the house, a flash of light can be seen inside the house through the bedroom window, followed by a yellow-and-blue glow. The light flickers on and off until, finally, the whole house is engulfed in a spectacular blaze of fire and light, with the sun like a spotlight on the house making it even brighter.

* * *

At the FDA office, Angela and Frank have the box from Dan's house out on a table going through it. Mike Brown and Troy Hanson from the FBI walk in.

"Mike, thanks for coming," Angela says. "I'm kind of at a loss here. We investigate companies and drugs, not crimes, and this is looking more and more like a crime."

"I didn't really understand the message you left me," Mike says. "I got that one of your people might be missing but did you say something about a vampire?" Mike laughs.

"Of course, there are no such things as vampires, but it's looking like Dan might think there is," Angela says.

"You're kidding, Dan is a solid guy," Mike says, "there's no way he went off the reservation."

"I would have never thought so, either, but this Old World case has hit him pretty hard," Angela says.

"Well, a parent never really quits grieving, no matter how long it's been," Mike says then glances at the papers in front of Frank and Angela on the table. "Let's see what you have here."

Mike walks over to the table and picks up a bullet with a silver tip to look at it. The rest of the group starts going through the papers on the table.

* * *

Azreal is sitting at his desk when Haley walks in and sits down in a chair on the other side of the desk.

"After we talked yesterday, I started asking around," Haley says, "and then I had security check the whole compound. Gabriel hasn't been here in days, and neither has Samantha."

Azreal leans back in his chair and puts his hands together again matching his fingertips up with each other, "Anyone knows where he might be? Did he say anything to Steven?"

"No, nothing," Haley says. "Steven hasn't seen them either"

"When was the last time you went to his house?" Azreal asks.

"I've intentionally avoided going there for a long time now, because I know I will see that his forest has grown," Haley says, looking concerned.

"Yes, I think we are both just as guilty of looking the other way when it comes to Gabriel's habits," Azreal says then stands and walks to the window.

"How long can we just keep ignoring it?" Haley says. "We both know that his forest is going to have more trees in it."

"You think he is the one reason for the recent disappearances, don't you?" Azreal asks.

"We've seen this before," Haley replies sadly. "I don't know how many times. We can't just keep hoping he stops. This time, we must do something about it."

"So, what are you suggesting we do?" Azreal asks.

"He needs to start over somewhere no one knows him," Haley says. "Somewhere less public." Haley continues. "A less developed country, where his indiscretions won't be noticed, and if there are, they can be bought off. South America, maybe?"

"So, you want me to send him away?" Azreal asks. "Just abandon him?"

"We aren't abandoning him, Azreal," Haley argues. "We are saving him again, and this time, we are saving ourselves too."

Azreal drops his head and puts his arm on the window frame to support himself. After thinking for a few moments Azreal responds. "You are right, this is the best thing for him and us. It finally must be done."

"We should go tonight," Haley says. "The sooner we address this with him, the better."

Azreal says. "We'll let Steven know on the way out that we will be gone for a few days." Then, they both walk out of Azreal's office and shut the door behind them.

* * *

CHAPTER FIFTEEN

The Year Is 2018

Angela, Mike, Troy, and Frank are sitting at the table in Angela's office, going over the papers from the Senator's box.

"Well, we don't really have anything here that doesn't sound-well, crazy," Mike says. "Let's go check out this Gabriel guy."

"Who knows?" Troy says, "We may get lucky."

* * *

Outside of Gabriel's house, Angela is sitting in the front seat of a car while Mike sits next to her in the driver's seat. Both of them focused in on Gabriel's massive, steel gated entrance.

The police radio crackles to life with Frank's voice, "A black Mercedes four-door just past us."

Mike picks up the radio mounted inside his car to respond but waits a second until he sees the Black Mercedes pull up to Gabriel's gate and stop. "10-4, we have eyes on it," Mike says into the radio. "Get ready to move, we are going in with that Mercedes."

"10-4, we are rolling now," Frank responds. "The steel gates start to open, and the Mercedes slowly move toward them and then past them as it enters the long driveway to Gabriel's estate.

"Move, move, slow, though," Mike can be heard over the radio, "we want them all the way inside the gates. No lights." Mike pulls out from the side of the road and follows, with Frank's car right behind him. No headlights; the cars blend into the night.

The gates close behind them. Mike and Frank pull their cars over as soon as they get inside the gates. The Mercedes continues up the driveway and comes to a stop behind Samantha's Mercedes, that is still in the driveway.

Gabriel swings open his front doors and steps out onto his driveway and into the cool night air. Azreal and Haley get out of their Mercedes and Azreal walks around the Mercedes to stand next to Haley in the driveway.

"So, you have both finally come to my home to see me, how nice," Gabriel says.

"Where have you been these last few days, Gabriel?" Azreal inquires.

"I have been here, Azreal," Gabriel says with a smile. "Why do you ask?"

"What have you been doing, Gabriel? And where is Samantha?" Haley asks.

"I have been here grieving, my friends," Gabriel says as his smile changes to an emotionless cold face.

"Grieving?" Azreal asks.

Gabriel walks out of his doorway and a few steps closer to Azreal and Haley, "Yes, grieving, and I have you two to thank for that! I would blame Samuel also, maybe then I would blame him the most, but he isn't around anymore for me to blame." .

"What are you talking about?" Azreal asks.

Gabriel stops and looks hard at Azreal and Haley for a few seconds, then breaks out into laughter and throws his hand in the air. "You two fools don't even know what has happened, do you?"

"Gabriel, we came here because we wanted to help you," Haley says.

Gabriel laughed again and then looks back at them with a crazy glazed look in his eyes, "No, Haley, you didn't come here to help me, and if you knew what happened, you really wouldn't be here for that. So, have you two seen Samuel lately? Did he say his goodbyes to you?"

Azreal and Haley look at each other wondering what Gabriel meant by his statement.

"From that look, I guess not," Gabriel says. "I thought for sure he would have at least said something to you, Azreal?"

"Did something happen to Samuel?" Azreal asks.

"You could say that," Gabriel says with a laugh. "I went to his house looking for someone to blame, but he beat me to it."

"What did you do!" Haley shouts.

"Unfortunately, I didn't do anything to him," Gabriel says. "Like I said he beat me to it. You two can stop by and look at what's left of his place."

"What happened, Gabriel?" Azreal asks.

"He finally did what he said he was going to all these years," Gabriel says. "Him and Emma are gone, and he is lucky he did it himself before I got to him!"

Azreal lowers his head in sorrow, “The Sun?”

“Absolutely!” Gabriel chuckles. “The house was just ashes and sticks when I got there.”

“Why did you go there?” Haley asks. “What happened to make you angry enough to want to hurt Samuel?

“You don’t need to worry about that FDA agent anymore, either,” Gabriel says.

“Fuck, Gabriel, you killed him, didn’t you?” Haley yells. “They will come looking for all of us!”

“Why, Gabriel?” Azreal asks. “Why would you do that?”

“He came here with Steven’s little friend Jacob and a crazy story that he had to have gotten for Myrick,” Gabriel says and starts making circles with both fingers pointing at his head like a crazy person.

“How do you know Myrick had anything to do with it?” Azreal asks.

“Because he came with a gun full of silver bullets!” Gabriel hisses. And then points straight at Azreal with his index finger. “That had to be Myrick. You two didn’t keep your deal with him, did you!”

"I was going to talk to you about him, but you never came in this week," Azreal says.

"He got a shot off before I know what he had in the gun," Gabriel says still looking at Azreal with crazy eyes.

"Dan?" Azreal asks.

"Yeah, Dan," Gabriel yells. "He killed Samantha right where your standing!"

"Samantha is gone, too?" Azreal asks.

From the bushes lining Gabriel's driveway, Troy and Mike emerge with their guns drawn and sighted in on Gabriel.

"I have heard enough!" Mike shouts at Gabriel. "Stop right where you are, you murdering son-of-a-bitch!"

From the bushes on the other side of the driveway closer to Azreal and Haley, Frank and Angela emerge from behind trees, guns drawn and pointed at them.

"Get on your knees, right now!" Mike shouts. "Downright now!"

"Did you bring more new friends?" Gabriel asks Azreal in a sinister voice.

"No, Gabriel we must have been followed," Azreal replies.

Azreal and Haley turn around to face Angela and Frank.

"Don't hurt them," Azreal yells to his companions!

"Azreal, you are on your own now!" Gabriel hisses back at him.

Gabriel turns and squares off with Mike, sizing him up quickly.

"I wish you would!" Mike yells. "I'm not going to tell you again! Get on your knees!"

"Angela, you have grown and done well, I'm happy for you," Azreal says.

"Get on your knees!" Angela shouts in response to Azreal. "Now! Now!"

"Angela, I don't want anything to happen to you, please lower your weapon and leave," Azreal says. "This can all be worked out."

Faster than light, Gabriel charges at Mike, grabbing his hands that are clenching his gun and with one powerful squeeze from Gabriel's hands Mike's hands are crushed, unable to control his gun it drops onto the ground. Gabriel spins around Mike and is behind him before and can move, forcing him to spin in a circle away from Troy, who is trying to stay sighted in on Gabriel with his gun. Ready to shoot at the first opportunity. They end up with Gabriel standing behind Mike with both of them looking at Troy. Mike is on his knees being choked by Gabriel now the same way he choked Dan and the same way he has chocked hundreds of others.

"Shoot!" Gabriel shouts at Troy, taunting him. While still crouched hiding behind Mike. "Go ahead and kill your friend!"

Azreal spins around to look at Gabriel, "Gabriel, stop!"

Gabriel slowly pulls a small silver bladed knife from under his jacket in his back waistband, that he had intended to use in killing Samuel earlier that night, he then raises it to Mike's throat.

"Gabriel, stop!" Azreal shouts again.

"You fool, it's too late for you to make this go away," Gabriel yells back to Azreal. "We must be what we truly are again!"

Gabriel looks over his shoulder at Azreal.

"Do it," Mike whispers to Troy as he struggles to breathe.

Gabriel is looking at Azreal when BOOM! A bullet from Troy's gun wizzes by the side of Gabriel's head, missing him by centimetres. Gabriel quickly looks back at Troy and another bang! The second bullet from Troy's gun finds a home deep in Gabriel's shoulder. Gabriel jerks back and involuntarily slice deep across Mike's throat with his knife.

Gabriel stumbles back a few feet, releasing Mike before catching his balance, and then focusing on Troy. Mike immediately grabs his throat with both hands, in an effort to stop a thick stream of blood squirting out of his throat with every fading heartbeat.

With the speed of a rocket, Gabriel lunges over Mike at Troy. Before Troy can process what is happening, Gabriel is on top of him, stabbing and slicing him, over and over and over so fast that Tony can't see where all the blows are coming from. Frank sights his gun in on Gabriel's back and pulls the trigger three times. BANG, BANG, BANG, all three bullets dig deep into Gabriel's back, forcing him to push forward. Gabriel spins around, looking back at Frank. Troy falls to the ground in a lifeless bloody mess on the driveway next to Gabriel.

"Stop!" Azreal shouts in desperation.

Haley seizes the opportunity, and in a split second, she quickly moves and rips Frank's gun out of his hand. Then, with the deliberate force of a hammer hitting a nail, Haley punches Frank in the center of his chest. Frank flies backwards, several feet in the air and lands hard on his back, holding his chest and trying to catch his breath, gasping for air.

Angela turns to look at Frank, then back to sight in on Haley. Azreal moves in and snatches her gun, before she knows he is there, then flings it deep into the bushes next to the driveway. Azreal pushes Angela back a few feet and onto the ground. Sensing Gabriel approaching fast from behind him, Azreal spins around and grabs Gabriel. One hand seizes his throat and the other on Gabriel's hand that is controlling his knife. With force and speed, Azreal lifts Gabriel up into the air and then slams him to the ground, still clenching Gabriel's throat like a vice-grip. Azreal quickly startles him with one knee on each side of him forcing Gabriel to remain on his back. Then slowly manipulates the hand, still holding the knife over the center of Gabriel's chest.

"It's okay, my brother," Gabriel says in a whisper to Azreal.

"Why are you making me do this?" Azreal cries back at him.

"You always knew it would have to end this way," Gabriel hisses. "I'm a monster, and I can never stop being that! No matter how hard you wish it, I will never stop being what I am."

Azreal looks up at the night sky and stars flickering in and out as he quickly forces Gabriel's hand to plunge the silver knife into his own chest. Azreal springs backward as Gabriel burst into a brilliant light of flames and then to dust and ashes.

Angela stands up and looks at Azreal, in disbelief of what she has just seen. With her mind still trying to process it all, she scans the area for her gun, that is lost in the bushes. Then back to look at Azreal again. Azreal stairs back deep into her eyes, unlocking a flood of memories and emotions that she tries to control. Slowly a lifetime of pictures of Azreal runs through Angela's mind. Angela walks a few steps closer to Azreal no longer fearing him, still confused she raises her hand and points her finger at him. "You, you're the man from the party," Angela says. "When I was just a little girl, you played ball with me. And I remember you carrying me."

Angela walks a few more steps toward Azreal to look at him closely in the moonlight. "I have seen you other times too. In the hospital when my mom was sick, I thought I saw you come out of her room and I passed you in the hallway." Angela continues. "That was the day my mom got better and was able to come home from the hospital, it was you…" Angela still moving closer, she is now only a foot away from Azreal. "And the day I graduated from high school..." Angela stops and looks down still recalling more and more images of Azreal flashing through her life. "The day I was promoted to Agent at the FDA, I saw you in the parking lot on the way to the ceremony… You have always been there."

Azrael looks at Angela and smiles as he opens his arms to embrace her.

THE END

About The Author

Brian Myrick was Born in Wasco, CA and lived most of his life in Bakersfield, CA. For the last twenty years Mr. Myrick has been a Federal Agent with the U.S. Government and has traveled extensively throughout the world doing assignments on behalf of U.S. Government. In addition to his federal service he is also a successful business person, owning a chain of bars and restaurants.

23903370R00105

Made in the USA
San Bernardino, CA
31 January 2019